Firestorm

A Jed McCain Mystery

Bill Cronin

Copyright

Dedication

To my wife, Linda.

Prologue

My dock is my refuge. When I rise in the morning and make coffee, I enjoy that first cup sitting at the end of the dock next to the Indian River and listening to the water lap against the pilings. The previous owner of my home had the foresight to build this dock to moor a twenty-seven-foot cabin cruiser he used for fishing three months during the winter. He didn't spend a nickel on the house, but he built this beautiful dock. It was the best money he ever spent. From here, I have a panoramic view of the waterfront. To the north, I can see past Chicken Island to the North Causeway. To the northwest, I have a view of the Coronado Beach city center, the city's marina, and the police station across the river. Brannon Center and Riverside Park are directly across the river from me. The South Causeway Bridge connecting the mainland and beachside arches over the river, dominating my view to the south.

This morning, sitting by the water reminds me of Battery Park at the southern tip of Manhattan, where the Hudson and East rivers converge. The panoramic view of Ellis Island, Governor's Island, the ports of New Jersey and the expanse of New York Harbor come to mind. I never tired of gazing upon the Statue of Liberty in the middle of the harbor. Those memories make me nostalgic for my days as a street cop and then a detective with the NYPD, when I'd find excuses on a pretty day to detour to Battery Park. While I still have the love of police work in my soul, my most fondly remembered days of being a police officer in New York

Firestorm

City were in the early 2000s following the terrorist attack on the Twin Towers. The city's chest swelled with patriotism, and young men and women lined up to join the police and fire departments. Being a cop meant something then. It was an honor to wear the uniform. I took pride in the work we did to keep the city safe and to bring criminals to justice.

It was a time when crime in New York was under control, in part due to controversial policies like stop and frisk and racial profiling, which resulted in a fifty-percent reduction in crime. As I approached twenty years of service with the NYPD, a political shift occurred, when those in power were more concerned about the rights of the criminal than they were about the victims. The police were villainized, as those in power not only rescinded stop and frisk and racial profiling but made significant strides to tie the hands of the police and drive a wedge between the police and the communities we served.

Did NYPD's aggressive enforcement go too far? Yes, I think it did. Was reform needed? Yes. But what happened in the later years of my service there was such a dramatic shift that the politicians and the public gradually came to view the police as the problem and not the solution. Crime in NYC is once again out of control. No longer are NYC police respected. Criminal elements gun down officers in our streets for little or no reason other than their cops. These officers put their lives on the line every day.

Then, there was a long waiting list for applicants to the NYPD police academy. Today, officers are retiring or quitting at a record rate, and the NYPD is unable to fill hundreds of vacancies for officers to replace them.

What has happened in NYC is an example of what has happened in the major metropolitan cities across America. As things go in NYC, so goes the rest of the country. The nation is struggling to find the balance between active enforcement of the laws and protecting the rights of the accused. It is a messy business.

As chief of the Coronado Police Department, I take pride that we've instituted reforms that protect the rights of the accused without losing sight of the rights of the victims. Is it easy? No. The lack of respect for police that's swept across our country has made its way to Coronado Beach. The public ridicules our officers, and routine domestic violence calls are an opportunity for someone to shoot one of our officers. Traffic stops turn into ugly confrontations.

The wind, though, is shifting. People are rising up in the face of unprecedented spikes in violent crime, demanding change. The same politicians who promoted defunding police are now advocating for a return to more rational policies. The pendulum is now moving toward supporting police and supplying resources we need. In restaurants that I frequent, I've more people coming up to me and thanking me for my service. I see the silent majority saying "Enough." Even with these encouraging signs, we still have a long way to go.

And criminal pressures aren't the only challenge I face as chief. While I report to the city manager, I serve at the pleasure of the city's council. In my three-year tenure, I've survived two close votes to have me removed from office. To say that my job is dangling from the thinnest of threads is an understatement. While a detective in the NYPD, I had to navigate the political storms of that job; nothing I experienced there prepared me for the political tightrope I walk daily here.

When I took the job, I'd applied for a position as a homicide detective. On the day I arrived, the previous chief resigned, and Neil Jarret, the city manager, pushed me into replacing Chief Grizzle. At the time, I really didn't want that responsibility. There were hard feelings on the part of senior officers in the PD who felt the city hadn't considered them for the position. The council was upset the city manager had hired me without giving the council the opportunity to interview me or propose candidates of their own. Jarret placed me in a job that no one wanted me in. Why? While Jarret had the authority to hire and fire, the Grizzle had friends and allies on the council. Although the chief reported to Jarret, Grizzle had routinely ignored him and relied on his relationships on the council to stay in power. Jarret wanted me because I had no political ties or affiliations with anyone. He wanted his own person in the chief's job. He thought that funneling all communications concerning police matters through him would reduce the political visibility of the police department and give the PD more room to run without political interference. While well intentioned, it was unworkable.

I live next door to the mayor, who befriended me the day I backed my trailer with all my belongings into the drive of my new home. In time, councilors began calling me directly when they felt that Jarret was withholding information from them. Jarret's view of these outside-the-chain-of-command communications were grounds for termination. And he fired me two years ago, giving me two weeks' notice. He reinstated me before the two weeks were up, but a tenuous truce has existed since. Fortunately, there hasn't been a major issue to test the limits of the relationship. There's no doubt another controversy will come. The only question is when.

As I finish my coffee, I consider why I remain in law enforcement and this job amid such hostile and often challenging circumstances. Lately, the thought of cashing out has occurred more often. Whenever I consider retirement, though, I always come to the same conclusion. I continue to wear the uniform because I think I can make a difference. When the day comes that I no longer feel that way, that's the day I'll turn in my shield.

Firestorm

1

"He's been missing for three days, Chief McCain."

The woman sitting across from me was attractive, in her late thirties. She had tied her medium brown hair into a ponytail and wore gym shorts, a tank top and bright lime green running shoes—athletic clothing a jogger might wear.

I opened the pencil drawer in my desk and removed a ballpoint pen. "What's his name?"

"Sebastian. Sebastian Sabatini."

I picked up a yellow legal pad, placed it on the blotter and printed his name on the first line. "Your name?"

"Katherine Grant."

"Your relationship to Mr. Sabatini?"

"I guess you'd describe me as his girlfriend." She sat perched on the edge of her chair, trying to read what I was writing on the pad. Her ponytail hung across her left shoulder and down her chest.

"You sound a little unsure of your relationship."

"That's because I've never been sure. But he calls me every day, and I haven't heard from him in three days."

"Does he live with you?"

"No, not regularly."

"What makes you so sure he's missing?"

"Aside from what I just told you, that he hasn't called me," she said with irritation, "I've gone by where he stays, and his car was there and, well, things didn't look right. There was no sign of him."

"Things didn't look right?"

"His car door was wide open, the keys were in the ignition, and his cellphones were lying on the passenger seat. My guess is that the car had been sitting for a while."

"What made you think that?" I asked.

"The battery was dead, probably from the open door."

"You say 'the place where he's staying' as though it's temporary."

"Sebastian is odd, Chief McCain. He refers to himself as a minimalist. That's his fancy name for a freeloader."

"You mean he's homeless?"

"Not homeless, exactly. He defines home on a day-by-day basis. He takes advantage of people's generosity. For example, take the two-acre place he's staying at now. He did investigative work for the woman who lives there in exchange for a place to park his travel trailer for a time. Once he finished his work, they agreed he'd move on. Only Sebastian wouldn't leave, and he forced her to evict him legally."

"I'm reading between the lines, but it sounds like this isn't the first time this has happened."

"No. It isn't. People have tried to help him, and he took advantage... No, that's not strong enough. He returned their generosity with abuse."

"Yet he's your boyfriend."

"Sebastian is a complex person, Chief. There are several sides to him. He can be charming and endearing. We built our relationship on that side of him; that's the part I fell in love with. He can also be difficult—exceedingly difficult—the reason I put limits on our relationship."

Firestorm

"What do you mean by difficult?" I asked.

"He has a violent temper. He's mean-spirited when he doesn't get his way. He seems to thrive on confrontation."

"Was he ever violent with you?"

"You mean did he ever hit me? No. He lost his temper with me several times, and I sent him packing. For some reason, he didn't retaliate."

"He did with others?"

"Yes."

"Do you think his disappearance is connected to the violent side of him?"

"Very much so. Something has happened to him."

"Have you considered your boyfriend left of his own accord? What if he doesn't want us to find him?"

"I don't think so."

"What makes you so sure?" I asked, tapping the pen on the desk blotter.

"He's a little agoraphobic as far as this area is concerned. His family is from New York, but he sees them infrequently. I've tried to get him to travel, but he's unwilling to leave his 'home,' as he calls it. Even though he has no home to speak of, the thought of him going somewhere else creates anxiety for him."

"You said your boyfriend was doing investigative work?"

"He's a licensed private investigator." Ms. Grant pulled out a picture from a small quilted handbag that hung across her shoulder and handed it to me. "I took this picture with my phone and printed it, so it is a little grainy."

Sabatini had a dark complexion and could have passed for someone from the Middle East. He was leaning against the driver's side door of a car with his arms folded over his chest. He hadn't shaved nor combed his thinning black hair and looked as if he'd just woken. Judging by his height in relationship to the car, he was over six feet tall, in his mid to late thirties and muscular. Wrinkled jeans, a T-shirt and soiled running shoes completed his unkempt appearance. His face was thin and angular, mouth small, nose long and thin, ears close to his head, and black eyebrows hung low over his eyes.

Ms. Grant leaned forward in her chair to look at the picture. "He doesn't look like much in that picture, but Seby—that's my name for him—is intelligent and engaging, when he wants to be."

I took a card out of the pencil drawer and handed it to her. "Could you text the picture to me? My cellphone number is on the bottom of the card."

Ms. Grant tapped the screen on her phone. "There, I sent it to you."

"What else can you tell me about him?"

"Sebastian is a private, secretive person. He talks about himself sparingly and changed the subject when I asked probing questions about his past, except when he ranted about his ex, or the people he felt were trying to hurt him."

"Ex?" I asked. "He was married?"

"Ex-girlfriend. Sebastian would never marry anyone. You should speak with her. He lived with her for six years."

"Do you think she might have had something to do with his disappearance?"

"I have no idea. I've only spoken to her once when Sebastian and I started dating."

"And?"

Firestorm

"She warned me about him. She specifically said that I shouldn't let him move in with me. She said that I'd regret it."

"Did you...let him move in?"

"No. He'd spend the night with me from time to time, but no, I didn't let him move in. I wasn't looking for a full-time companion. I've had two spectacularly awful marriages, Chief. I was not in the market for another. I like my independence."

"Do you have the ex's name?"

"Jane Frost." She reached into her purse and pulled out two pieces of paper. "Here is Jane's information."

I looked at the first piece of paper with a handwritten address on it. Her residence was on beachside, off Flagler Avenue. The city of Coronado Beach was divided by the Indian River. Locals referred to the part of town west of the river as mainland and the barrier island east of the river as beachside.

"She works In Daytona somewhere, at an attorney's office, I think. I don't know where." Ms. Grant handed me the second piece of paper. "This is the address and phone number of his parents. They live in Beacon, New York."

Beacon was up the Hudson River from New York City. I'd been there on business with the NYPD.

I asked, "Have you contacted them?"

"Yes. I reached out to them to see if they'd heard from him. I learned that he called his father every day. When his father told me he hadn't heard from Sebastian either, I decided to come to you. They're on their way down now. They're worried sick."

"Why me? Why didn't you call 911?"

"Ashley... I mean Ms. Rand suggested I come to see you. I work in her office as a paralegal. She suggested that if I spoke to you, it might have a higher priority."

Ashley Rand was an attorney in Coronado Beach whom I'd been seeing for the last seven months. I looked down at my notes.

"You said Sabatini has a violent temper and that he is confrontational."

"He thrives on confrontation, Chief McCain."

"Do any names come to mind of people who would want to harm him?"

"Every day he told me about this person or that he'd gone off on. There were so many, I hardly paid attention. One incident, over a year ago, that I do remember had to do with your police department. One of your patrol officers pulled him over for a minor infraction. Sebastian claimed that your officer assaulted him and put him in jail. When they released him, he filed a complaint with the department and one with the Florida Department of Law Enforcement. I also remember bailiffs escorting him out of the clerk of court's office in Deland after a belligerent confrontation he had with the clerk over a restraining order he'd filed against someone. He was fearless. He angered scores of people, Chief."

"And you think he took on the wrong person?"

"Yes."

"You found his car. Where was he staying?"

"On a piece of property on the edge of town." She gave me the address.

"Did you touch the cellphones you said you found in the car?"

Firestorm

"No. I didn't touch anything, except to close the door of his car."

"We will need to get your fingerprints," I said.

"I understand."

"You said you found two phones?"

"Yes. I didn't know that he had two."

"And you say he had a trailer on the property?"

"Yes, one that hitches to the bumper of a car. A small one."

"Did you have a key?"

"No. I've never been in it. I've only been out there twice. Once when we were going out somewhere and he forgot his wallet, and the second time when I found his abandoned car."

I looked at my notes, which had filled two pages on my legal pad. "All right. I'll have more questions, but this should get me started."

"Behind all the bluster and anger, I've never seen him hurt anyone. He could throw a tantrum, and he could be mean, but I don't think he'd physically hurt anyone unless someone tried to hurt him."

I stood, and so did Ms. Grant. She extended her hand, and I shook it.

"Thanks, Chief McCain."

"I'll be in touch when I've something to report." As she turned to leave, I said, "One more thing."

She turned and faced me.

"How did you and Sabatini meet?"

"He does investigative work for our law firm from time to time."

"Ashley Rand's firm?"

"Yes. But it was her ex-husband, Eddy, who hired him. Ashley, I mean Ms. Rand, rarely gets involved in criminal cases."

2

Sergeant Martha Johnson, my assistant, found the empty chair just vacated by Katherine Grant in my office. Six months ago, her only son Deshon had become ensnared in a city-boy gang in Daytona. He had been due to testify against the gang who had beaten an elderly man to death as part of a gang initiation. Three gang members had gunned down Deshon and two Daytona Beach police officers in a safe house before he could testify.

Johnson had returned from leave following her son's death sans attitude or the in-your-face style that had endeared her to the command staff. While she continued to run the department and executed her considerable responsibilities with professionalism, I knew a part of her had died when the gang had taken her son's life. She'd encouraged Deshon to "do the right thing" and testify. Now she blamed herself for his death, and no amount of persuasion could extract her from that hell. At just over five feet tall, Johnson had lost sixty pounds and looked gaunt, her uniform nearly sagging on her, and she appeared older than her years. I missed the Johnson who would stand at the door to my office, hands on her ample hips, and chew my ass for some small infraction of protocol, or tell me I could kiss her ass if I asked her to get me coffee or requested something from her she felt was beneath her dignity. My heart bled for her.

"I heard that woman mention Sebastian Sabatini," she said.

"You heard that from your cubicle."

"I'm the assistant to the chief. Nothing gets past me."

"Apparently not."

"The department has a long history with Mr. Sabatini, Chief. Before you go a step further, you should talk to Carl Stanton. He nearly lost his job over Sabatini."

"All right. Ms. Grant just asked me to open a missing person case on Sabatini. He's disappeared."

"Good riddance as far as the department is concerned. The FDLE was up Grizzle's ass on that one."

"What happened?"

"Following two months of investigation, FDLE didn't find anything that substantiated Sabatini's claim, and the city dropped the matter. However, Grizzle was under pressure to fire Stanton and his partner, and Mr. Jarret was having a fit over it. Mr. Jarret didn't think much of our chief then."

"Would you find Commander Downs for me?" I asked.

Johnson pointed behind me to the phone on my credenza, stood up from her seat and left my office. At least she didn't totally ignore me. It wasn't a "kiss my ass," but it was close. A good sign she was on the mend.

Commander Leslie Downs, head of the investigations division of the department, which included a squad of detectives and crime scene investigators, was tall, slender and athletically built. Her cubicle was in a corner on the second floor of the PD, wedged in by a dozen or more empty military surplus desks crammed together into a bullpen for her detectives. Downs was on the phone when I rounded the corner to her cube. She held up her index finger and hurried the conversation she was having, then hung up.

"What's up?" She spun around in her chair to face me, and she instantly saw my reaction to her haircut. Downs had had long light red hair that hung to the middle of her back. Now it was short with pointed sideburns, and the cut tapered at the neck. "I got tired of messing with it," she said.

The week before, during an arrest, a perp had grabbed her by her hair and nearly got the best of her.

I handed her the piece of paper with the address where Sabatini had been living that Ms. Grant had given me. "His girlfriend reported him missing. I need a warrant to search his car and a travel trailer he owns parked at that address."

"You sure you want to do this? You know who this guy is, don't you?"

"No, but obviously everyone else does."

"Sabatini isn't worth the department's time or trouble. You execute a search warrant on his property, and I guarantee you he'll sue you and me and anyone else connected to it. I'm not even sure I can find a judge who'll stick his neck out and issue one."

"All the more reason to have a search warrant. Do your best."

Even though major cases came under Downs' responsibilities, she and I worked those cases together as partners. It was not that Downs was incapable. She was an excellent investigator. I had grudgingly accepted the position of chief, but in truth, I loved detective work. Fortunately, Downs and I made a good team, and she enjoyed the camaraderie as much as I did.

Firestorm

"When do you want to execute the warrant?" she asked.

"ASAP. I have Officer Stanton coming into the PD now."

"You picked the right guy. He'll give you an earful." She tried to flip her non-existent long hair over her shoulder, caught herself and said, "This will take some getting used to." She smiled.

"It looks good," I lied. "Call me when you're ready to roll."

Six-foot two-inch Sergeant Carl Stanton stood at attention and filled the doorway to my office. I motioned for him to grab a chair.

Once he sat down, I said, "Relax. Everything is fine. I just need background on a reported missing person." Stanton had the body of a weightlifter. With his blond crew cut and smooth face, he looked ten years younger than his thirty-nine years. He'd been an MP in the Marine Corps, retired after 20 years, completed the police academy and been hired on here three years ago as a police officer.

"Sabatini," he said, as one might invoke the name of the devil.

"Yes. Fill me in."

"My partner and I were on patrol and observed a car with an expired tag. We pulled the car over, got out of the cruiser, and I asked the driver for his license. The guy, Sabatini, said, 'I'm not giving you a fucking thing. I haven't done anything wrong.'

"I explained to him that he had an expired tag, and before I could finish explaining why we'd stopped him, he bolted from the car and tried to hit me with his car door. Then he goes into this rage, asking, 'don't you have anything better to do than harass people over petty bullshit?' I again asked him for his license, and I told him to get back into his car.

"Then he flies into a rage again, screaming at us that he was going to file a complaint and that we'd be sorry we'd ever pulled him over, that we'd no idea who we were messing with. He became so aggressive, I ordered him back into his car or we'd cuff him. It was then that he shoved me, and it took both my partner and me to restrain him. I cuffed him, put him in the back of the cruiser, had his car towed to an impound yard, and charged him with assaulting a police officer. On the way to the station, he was screaming continuously, calling us every expletive you can imagine. We added 'resisting' to the charges.

"Then the shit hit the fan when we placed him in a holding cell. He was yelling that I'd assaulted him. That we'd yanked him out of the car and brutally cuffed him because he'd asked why we stopped him. He demanded to talk to the chief and screamed that we were violating his rights. He said he was going to sue the department and me personally.

"We called Grizzle just to get the guy to shut up. That was a huge mistake. All Sabatini had to say was that he was going to sue Grizzle, and Grizzle let him go. He didn't even listen to what we had to say. He just let him go. He even apologized to that bastard. Can you believe it?

"Then Sabatini files a complaint anyway with the department and the FDLE that I assaulted him. Grizzle suspended me and my partner without pay for two months until he could 'resolve the matter.' Grizzle had the city manager convinced that we'd overreacted. It wasn't until Jim Cahill with the FDLE interviewed my partner and me separately that he confirmed that Sabatini had an expired tag. He interviewed Sabatini himself and concluded that we were telling the truth and that it was Sabatini who'd in fact assaulted us. Grizzle restored us to duty but never paid us back pay or apologized. By then, the chief was unwilling to go after Sabatini, preferring to 'let sleeping dogs lie.'"

I said, "From listening to people in the department, it sounds like we've had multiple run-ins with him."

"I had another run-in with him two months after the PD put me back on duty. A retired female police officer from Orlando PD lives on beachside and called 911 about a suspicious vehicle parked in the alley behind her house. She lived alone and was concerned for her safety. When we rolled up into the alley, I recognized Sabatini's car. When I turned the spotlight on, Sabatini got out of his car, hopping mad. I got out of the cruiser and made sure he didn't get within ten feet of me. I asked him what he was doing in the alley and told him we had a complaint about him.

"He said it was none of our effing business. That it was a public alley and he'd every right to park in it. I told him that while that may be true, we'd every right to remain there with him. I turned on the blue lights, and we waited him out. After five minutes or so, he got back in the car, stuck his arm out the window, flipped me the bird and drove off. I didn't learn until later that he was stalking his ex-girlfriend, who lived five houses down from where he parked."

"Stalking his ex?"

"All the info I can give you is incomplete. His ex-girlfriend sent him packing, and he didn't take her throwing him out very well. He set up a camp behind a vacant house next door and harassed her. She filed a restraining order, and dispatch sent us to her house multiple times to deal with him. Grizzle was afraid of him and never let us do anything more than enforce the order to the letter."

"Was he ever arrested?"

"No. Like I said, Grizzle was afraid of him. You need to talk to the ex. She'll give you an earful."

"Is that it?"

"No. Sabatini careened from one interpersonal disaster to another. The slightest affront would ignite him; a take-no-prisoners situation would erupt. He was on fire, Chief, and burned everyone around him. Every officer in the department has crossed paths with him over the last two or three years."

"Anyone stand out that would want to do him harm?"

Stanton raised an eyebrow. "You're serious? If he *is* missing, my guess is he messed with the wrong person. Good luck with finding that person. The list of suspects would go around the block. I'd start with the ex. Sabatini put her through hell."

3

Leslie Downs secured a search warrant for the address provided by Katherine Grant. Downs and I took an unmarked cruiser to the address. A chain-link fence surrounded the grounds, and a mangled, unhinged ten-foot-wide wire gate stood cockeyed at the opening. Inside the gate, the sandy driveway branched, one path leading to the mobile home and the other to the other side of the property, where we could barely make out a car and trailer through the trees and underbrush.

Hundred-year oaks bedecked with Spanish moss surrounded a double-wide mobile home that hugged the back of the property. A crudely constructed wooden porch with two folding lawn chairs fronted the mildew-covered, vinyl-clad structure. Someone had parked a rusted mid-nineties compact car near the porch.

Downs and I ascended the porch, and I knocked on the door. No response. Then I knocked a second time with more force before a woman in her early thirties answered, walked out of the front door, and stood on the porch with her arms folded over her ample chest. She wore a white tank top, gym shorts and flip-flops. She was of medium height and had deep brown shoulder-length hair, and tattoos covered both arms. "You're here about Sebastian."

Downs said, "We have a missing person report and a warrant to search his possessions on your property." Downs proffered the warrant, but the woman waved her off.

"I'd prefer that you take all his junk with you when you leave. I served him with an eviction order, but he refused to go. Now you say he's missing?"

"We don't know if he's missing or not," I answered. "That's what we're checking into. May we have your name, ma'am?"

"Paula Cane."

"Do you own the property, Ms. Cane?"

"Yes, me and the bank." She chuckled at her own joke.

Downs asked, "What can you tell us about Mr. Sabatini?"

"I don't know where to begin.".

I suggested to Cane that we go inside, where she could tell us her story.

"No. My baby girl is in her rocker, and I just got her to sleep." She paused for a moment. "I regret the day I ever tried to help that little shit." Cane moved over to one of the lawn chairs and sat down in a heap.

I motioned to Downs to take the remaining chair, and I leaned against the rickety porch rail.

"I met Sebastian while I was in the process of divorcing my ex-husband. I couldn't prove my husband was cheating on me. A friend of mine had used Sabastian, and suggested I call him, that he'd barter in exchange for his services."

"What kind of services?" I asked.

"Private investigator. He came to the house and said he'd be happy to help me. He told me he was a former police officer and needed a place to park his camper for a month. He offered to surveil my ex in exchange for a place to park the camper. I agreed. That was the biggest mistake of my life." She swatted a mosquito away from her face. "He never mentioned, nor did I anticipate, that 'parking his camper' "—she raised her hands and made air quotes—"meant him living in it. That should have been a sign to me. When he produced pictures and documentation of the affair my ex was having, I didn't want to appear ungrateful by telling Sebastian that living in the camper was not part of the deal. When the month was up, though, he didn't leave. I waited and caught him late one evening and told him his month was over and I expected him to move on. He told me that the information he'd given me on my ex was worth far more than a month of rent. When I told him that was not what we'd agreed to, he flew into a rage and, yelling at the top of his lungs, he said that he was staying-—that there was nothing I could do to stop him. He told me I'd invited him to move his camper onto my property, that there was no written agreement between us, and on the issue of the length of the stay, it was his word against mine. From that evening forward, he made my life a living hell." She wiped tears from her eyes.

I asked, "So you did nothing?"

Her face reddened with anger. "My friend is a sheriff's deputy with Volusia County. He said the only way to get Sabatini out of here was by serving him with an eviction notice. I got a lawyer. It cost me every dime of my savings. I taped the eviction notice to the door of his camper. When he found it, he banged on my door. When I opened it, he exploded. He called me a slut and a whore and told me I'd regret the day I crossed him. He told me I had no idea who I was dealing with. He ripped the eviction notice up in front of me and threw it in my face."

"What happened then?" I asked.

"I went inside and called my boyfriend. He told me not to have anything to do with Sebastian. That he'd take care of it."

"Did you notice Sabatini was missing?"

"No."

"When was the last time you saw him?"

"When he threw the eviction notice in my face."

"When was this?"

"Three or four days ago."

"Did you notice that his car door was open?" I asked.

"No. I noticed that he parked his car there the last few days. He's usually out of here before I go to work. After my latest encounter, I didn't want to be anywhere near him."

"Did you see him get into a car with someone?"

"No. I'm gone during the day. I'm a nurse. I work the day shift in the emergency room at the hospital four days a week, and if we're busy, I often work until seven or eight at night."

"Have you seen anything that might explain his disappearance?"

"No. I'm sorry. You're welcome to search his things, but I don't know anything more than I've told you. If you don't mind, I need to check on my baby."

"For the record, could you give us the name of your sheriff friend?" I asked.

"Why do you want to talk to him?"

"You relied on him for advice. He could offer us a perspective that could be helpful."

Firestorm

She gave us the name and phone number of of Sergeant Malcolm Hicks.

As Downs and I were walking to Sabatini's car, she said, "She seemed pretty nervous."

"Yep. It could be Sabatini has her spooked, or she could know more than she's telling."

The car, an older Toyota Camry, sat next to an old Shasta travel trailer shaped like a canned ham on wheels. Downs and I surveyed the area. Sabatini had parked the trailer on the left rear corner of the property, four hundred feet from Cane's mobile home, under another antique oak tree. The Toyota sat on a bare patch in the thin grass near the entry door to the camper.

Downs said, "You said the car door was open when his girlfriend was here?"

"Yes." I approached the car. I looked inside the driver's side window and saw two cellphones sitting on the passenger seat.

"We should get Torres out here with her crew." Downs pulled her cellphone out of her pants pocket and made the call.

Alicia Torres was head of the newly acquired crime lab crew. When the FDLE had shuttered their Daytona Beach bureau and their crime lab, the Coronado Beach PD had hired their entire staff, a move that had not been without political controversy.

I looked at the driveway and saw at least three sets of tire tracks near the car, blended in among leaf debris from the oak trees in the yard. Three tracks stopped short of the car and were different from the tire tracks from the road to the camper.

Downs looked in the car window. "The keys are in the ignition." She walked back behind the car and squatted over the tire tracks. Then she got up and hiked over to our cruiser parked close to Cane's double-wide trailer.

"Jed, come look at this."

I walked over to where she had crouched to examine our tracks.

She said, "One of the tracks over by Sabatini's car is a match for our cruiser tires."

"How did you know that?"

"I've worked enough crime scenes where I had to eliminate our police vehicles' tire tracks. The tread that comes with the tires of our Ford Police Interceptor have a unique design. I've seen enough of them to recognize it."

I looked at the tread marks where she was squatting near our cruiser, then we fast-walked back to near Sabatini's car, where one of the tracks matched our cruiser.

Downs walked from Sabatini's car to Cane's car and examined that tire tread, then walked back to where I was standing, careful not to step on tire prints. "Her tires don't match any of the treads over here."

I said, "So out of the three tread marks, one matches our cruiser, one matches Sabatini's car and the other is unknown. So that leaves one unexplained tire tread, this one, which comes closest to Sabatini's car. See how the unexplained tread covers the others? It was the last vehicle to enter the area."

Downs said, "Cane just told us her friend was a sheriff's deputy. Both our PD and the Sheriff's Department use Ford Police Interceptor sedans. I'd be interested to know what kind of patrol car her friend drives. I'll have Torres' team process the scene and make casts of all the tire tracks."

Firestorm

"Katherine Grant said she'd driven out to check on Sabatini. Maybe that last track belongs to her car."

"I'll have someone take an impression of her tire."

"What do you make of it?" I asked.

"This looks like an abduction to me. If it had been a robbery, the two cellphones would have been gone, and someone would have stolen the car. The fact that the door was open tells me he left with someone and couldn't secure his vehicle. If he was a private investigator, his phone would have been important enough to take with him."

"That's what I'm thinking. The only other explanation would be that Sabatini staged the scene to look like an abduction so that he could disappear."

"Maybe," Downs said. "We can't rule that out."

I walked toward the extremely faded yellow and white trailer. The camper was sixteen feet in length, its exposed steel surfaces thick with rust. One tire on the passenger side was flat and weather-checked. Jalousie windows covered in mold and tree debris indicated the trailer's age and lack of care. I tried the door. Someone must have used a crowbar on the door because they'd destroyed the door jamb. I looked over at Downs, paused and then pulled it open.

The inside of the trailer smelled of rotten wood, the vinegary odor of dirty laundry, and soiled bedclothes. The paneled plywood walls were delaminated from water intrusion and coated in mildew in places, and, as I stepped inside, I found the floor was soft around the door from water damage. I moved toward the rear to make room for Downs. There was enough room for both of us to stand in the center of the trailer but not by much.

"She said he lived in this?" Downs looked first at the small booth in the front, then the small galley, which consisted of a tiny sink, a refrigerator the size of a mini-bar in a hotel and a two-burner propane stovetop. A platform double bed with cabinets underneath consumed the back. Right next to the entry door was a clothes closet as narrow as a filing cabinet. There was no bathroom.

While the camper reeked of decay, it was neat, and Sabatini had made the bed. He had outfitted the booth like a desk. There was a Coleman lantern on the booth table, confirming the lack of electricity. It reminded me of Katherine Grant's description of Sabatini as a minimalist. There were several open file boxes on the floor and manila folders scattered over the bed, table and galley counter. It was obvious that someone had been looking for something.

Downs broke the silence. "This is like living in a closet."

"I guess it's better than living on the street or in your car," I said.

"Not by much."

"Why don't you wait for Torres and her crew? After they process the scene, I want them to take the camper and car to the crime lab and dust everything for prints. Once they do that, I want you to go through all these files and determine if there's anything that can give us a clue as to Sabatini's whereabouts. I'm going to track down Malcolm Hicks. While you're waiting on Torres, could you get background on Hicks for me before I meet with him?"

I left the trailer, and as I was getting ready to leave, Paula Cane walked to the cruiser.

Firestorm

"When can you get his trailer and car off of my property?"

"As soon as the crime lab finishes their work, I'll have his things moved to an impound yard, later today."

"Thanks... What was your name?"

"Jed McCain."

As I was closing the door to the car and Cane made her way back to her trailer, Downs caught me. "I phoned Katherine Grant, and she confirmed that she'd driven to Sabatini's trailer and parked behind his car yesterday."

As I left the scene, I'd no faith we'd find Sabatini based on a tired tread. While the manufacturer installed the tire in question on the Ford Interceptor, they also installed them on several other Ford models. It was a long shot at best.

4

As I left Paula Cane's property, I called the Volusia County sheriff, as a courtesy, to let him know that I wanted to interview Hicks about the Sabatini disappearance. We agreed that Hicks would meet me at our PD. He said that Hicks was one of his finest officers. Since the Sheriff's Department sub-station was within a block of the PD, Hicks was leaning up against his cruiser, waiting for me as I pulled into the PD parking lot. As I parked the unmarked car, Downs called me.

"This is a summary of what I could find on Hicks. If you want more, it will take time."

I said, "Give me what you have."

"Hicks enlisted in the Army after September eleventh. He served for four years and achieved the rank of sergeant. He served two tours of duty in Iraq, and on his second tour, he received a Silver Star for bravery.

"This guy is the genuine article. When he got out of the Army, he enrolled at Daytona Community College and received a two-year degree in criminology with honors. He then graduated from the Volusia County Police Academy at the top of his class. He's been in the force for nine years and made sergeant during his second year. Last year, the Sheriff's Department awarded him the medal of valor and a purple heart for his actions responding to a domestic disturbance call where the armed suspect fired a shotgun at him, and Hicks sustained minor injuries. His record is impeccable. Do you need more?"

Firestorm

I said, "Not for now. I got the picture."

I disconnected with Downs, got out of the car and walked across the parking lot, where Hicks was pacing back and forth by his patrol car. I noticed immediately that he was driving a newer Ford Taurus Police Interceptor the same year and model as my unmarked car.

As I approached Hicks, I was impressed with his size. It wasn't that he was terribly tall, but he was large through his chest and arms, emphasized by the Kevlar vest he wore. His hair was black, cut in military fashion, short on top and cut close to the skin above his ears. He'd a neatly trimmed black mustache and a thick five o'clock shadow.

As I approached him, I held out my hand, and he took it and returned a firm handshake.

"Sergeant Hicks?"

"Yes, sir."

"Jed McCain. I want to ask you about Sabastian Sabatini."

"Yeah, the Sheriff told me you wanted to talk about him."

"Do you want to go inside to my office or talk here?"

"We're shorthanded today, and I'm the only deputy covering this area. Could we just talk here so I can respond to a call?"

I looked at the Pirelli tires on his cruiser, and they matched the tread we'd found near Sabatini's car.

I said, "We're investigating the possibility that Sabatini may be missing."

"Paula Cane called me about your visit."

"What's your relationship with Paula Cane?"

"I met Paula at the hospital when I brought one of my patrol officers to the ER for a nasty cut he got on his arm arresting a drunk at a domestic disturbance.. Paula was an ER nurse on duty. She'd just filed for divorce, and since I'm in the middle of a divorce, we swapped horror stories. One thing led to another, and we started spending time together. She used Sabatini to investigate an affair her husband was having. Paula told me she filled you in on the details."

"Are you involved with Paula Cane?"

"If you're asking whether we're having a physical relationship, we aren't. I'm fond of her, and we've developed a close friendship that I hope develops into something more. I've been to her home several times and spent hours with her, talking about our divorces."

"When was the last time you were at her house?"

"I was there two days ago, the afternoon Sabatini threw the eviction notice in Paula's face. Paula called me in hysterics after he threatened her and refused to leave."

"It sounds like there's more to this than you're saying."

"After I got to Paula's when my shift ended and I saw how distraught she was, I went to Sabatini's trailer, called him out and told him that if he knew what was good for him, he'd have the trailer off the property by nightfall. Then he threatened me. He told me that he knew about my divorce and that the judge in the case would be extremely interested in my comings and goings at Paula's house. He said if I interfered, he had pictures of me hugging Paula on the porch that he'd send to both my wife and the court. While the picture doesn't show anything, they could draw inferences from it."

"And?"

"You're going to find out anyway..."

"What happened?"

"While he was threatening me, he started poking me in the chest and pushing me. I lost it. I took the little shit apart and tuned him up good. I pulled him up off the ground by his shirt and told him if I came back the next day and he was still on Paula's property, the beating I'd just given him would be kid's play."

"This was three days ago?"

"Yes."

"And did you come by yesterday?"

"Yes. His car and trailer were still there. Someone left the front door of his car open, and it looked suspicious, so I left it. I called Paula and told her under no circumstances was she to go near Sabatini's trailer."

"Did you alert the police to your suspicions?"

He looked everywhere but at me. "Look, I'd just taken Sabatini over the hurdles. I wasn't keen about trying to explain my actions." He looked straight at me. "I can tell you Sabatini was alive and well when I left him. If he's missing, I had absolutely nothing to do with it."

I said, "We found tire tracks matching the tread to your cruiser in front of Sabatini's car and trailer."

"Paula and I were seeing one another on the down-low. If I took my sheriff's vehicle to her house, it would be like taking out a full-page ad in the newspaper. I never brought the county's vehicle anywhere near Paula's property."

"And when you 'tuned up' Sabatini, as you put it, how did you get to the property?"

"My own personal vehicle."

"And where did you park?"

"Near Paula's mobile home."

"And you have no idea what happened to Sabatini?"

"There's no telling. He was evil incarnate, Chief. With every breath he took, he created an enemy. All I can tell you is that he was alive when I left, and I've no idea what happened to him after that. I know how it looks, but I'm giving it to you straight."

I thanked him for meeting with me and shook his hand.

Hicks asked, "What'll happen now?"

"I want an impression of the tires on your patrol car. Beyond that, I don't have anything more for you now. But until we find Sabatini, you're not in the clear, Sergeant."

"I understand."

Firestorm

5

Jim Cahill was the special agent in charge of the Orlando bureau of the FDLE. He was in his mid-forties, not overly tall, with a full head of neatly clipped, dark wavy hair parted in the middle of his head. His closely trimmed black mustache and eyebrows set against a tanned face enhanced his having-it-together persona. He had expensive taste in suits and looked more presidential than a SAC.

In the three years that I'd been at Coronado Beach PD, he'd become a mentor, colleague and friend. Cahill's singular recommendation to Neil Jarret had secured my employment with CBPD, first as a homicide investigator, and now as chief. Unless he was directly involved in a major case, we'd meet for lunch every other week and for drinks every Monday night.

On occasional Mondays, Jim's beautiful wife Sandy, who worked in publicity at NASCAR in Daytona, would join us. Sandy found my bachelor status untenable and had made it her mission to connect me with one of the single, out-of-my-league models who orbited NASCAR promotions. I had demurred. After several attempts, she had given up and gave me a good-natured tough time whenever we got together.

Today, it was lunch at the Half Wall, a sports bar restaurant on Highway 44. Anyone who spent any time with Cahill knew that he was destined for senior management with FDLE. FDLE had promoted him to head the bureau in Orlando six months ago, and he was on the fast track to anywhere he wanted to go. I was impressed with his command of people, envious of his political skills and a willing follower of his enormous confidence. Yet beyond all of Jim Cahill's talents, the qualities that most endeared him to me were his genuine, humble nature and his unwavering loyalty. I could think of nothing I'd done to earn the latter, but it has become an invaluable thread in the fabric of our friendship.

Half Wall, by Coronado Beach standards, offered decent food at reasonable prices and booths in the dining room where you could converse without yelling.

I began, "Explain to me why I can't stay away from investigations."

"Why? What're you working on now?" he asked.

"A missing person case."

"What's it been, a year since you pulled that girl off Disappearing Island? You're bored."

"No, it isn't boredom."

"Sure it is."

"There's work to do. I just..."

"You're bored. Admit it."

I looked at my friend for a moment. He had a shit-eating grin on his face. "I like the job and the freedom I have, but I miss the work. I miss the streets."

"If you had the opportunity to go back to the NYPD, would you take it?"

"No. That's easy."

"Would you be happier if you'd remained a homicide investigator and not taken the chief's job?"

"No, not enough to do. I'd be working B&Es and robberies. That's boring grunt work."

Firestorm

"Well, you could always come to work for FDLE. I have plenty for you to do."

"Too much politics," I said.

"You think there's too much politics at Fiddle? I can't count the hours I spend dealing with small-town PDs and sheriff's department politics. This year, corrupt city or county elected officials have brought six chiefs up on unfounded charges. It's the Wild West out there, Jed. Coronado Beach is Pleasant Valley compared to the hellholes I'm called into. You don't know how good you have it. I'll say one thing about Grizzle. He knew the political side of being a chief. He may have stunk at everything else, but he knew how to manage the city council and suck up to community leaders."

"Yeah, and that got him sideways with Jarret."

"Your pledge not to go around the city manager to the mayor and council—how is that working?"

"Good. I hate politics. He's good at it, and I'm not."

"You still need to build a positive relationship with the council. You never know when you'll need it. Look at Bill Lee, the chief in Sanford, Florida."

"The Trayvon Martin case?"

"The city manager fired Lee after the city commission unanimously voted no confidence in his continued employment. While he may not have done anything legally wrong, the nation-wide negative publicity the city received over his handling of the investigation, and the protests that rocked the city for weeks, gave the politicians little choice but to let him go."

"What you're saying is I'm one crisis away from losing my job?"

"You've been here a little over three years, and the council has nearly fired you twice. If it weren't for your personal relationship with the mayor, you'd be fishing off your dock full time. You may need support from those council members one of these days. Didn't you tell me McFarland wants to retire?"

"Yeah, but Jarret is pressing him to remain."

"Still. Within the bounds of commitments you've made to Jarret, you need to build support on the council."

I took a sip of my Coke and looked up at one of a dozen TV screens showing a replay of the Yankees/Red Sox game. Much to the displeasure of my friends at the NYPD, I was a Red Sox fan and was pleased to see the Yankees down two at the top of the ninth.

I asked Cahill, "What're you working on now?"

"I can't give you details, but it's a gambling ring that pays our officers to look the other way. Watch the news over the next few days."

"Wouldn't that be an issue for Internal Affairs?"

"Yes, if the department was large enough. But when they aren't or when the corruption involves senior officers and the public could question the integrity of the investigation, we get involved."

"I heard one estimate when I was with the NYPD that at any given time, ten percent of the department, from the cop on the street to senior staff, were on the take in one form or another. That true?"

"Hard to say. It wouldn't surprise me. In Florida, we pay police officers barely a livable wage. When a motorist offers a cop a fifty to avoid a two hundred dollar speeding ticket, it can be hard to turn down. Imagine the temptation when gangs offer police thousands to keep a meth factory under the radar. It's a constant issue."

I was surprised how little CBPD paid its officers and staff compared to what NYPD paid its department. Jarret had explained to me that he did a survey of all the police and sheriff's departments and tried to keep our wages slightly above average. The city ran lean, and the conservative council was loath to increase taxes.

"Nobody wants corruption, but no one wants to do the things necessary to remove the temptation, like paying a decent wage," Cahill said.

Our server delivered our food, and between bites, Cahill and I discussed how poorly the Marlins were performing, how great it would be when college football returned and our common hatred of the Yankees.

As I drove back to the PD, I admitted to myself that while I was pleased that the last six months had been relatively quiet at the department, I missed the fire-drill atmosphere at the NYPD that had marked most days, and the daunting challenge of working multiple homicide cases under some of the most hostile conditions. Sarah James, my former boss, had understood the attraction to the work and could relate to the daily buzz of working under extreme pressure. Unfortunately, she was gone, murdered by the Night Fire Strangler. Though I tried as hard as I could, even though my relationship with attorney Ashley Rand had become more intimate, I couldn't get past the enormous loss of Sarah. At a point when I had realized how much I'd loved her, the Strangler had taken her from me.

6

When I got back to the PD and my office, Martha Johnson announced that Sebastian Sabatini's parents were in the lobby and wanted to meet with me. I asked her to call Leslie Downs and tell her I'd like her to sit in on the interview. Shortly, Johnson escorted the elderly parents into my office, made the introductions and closed the door as she left.

I gestured to vacant chairs around the conference table. "Please."

The woman was in her mid-fifties and heavyset with gray-flecked black hair pulled into a casual bun, deep brown bags under her brown eyes, and a faint mustache. She wore a black dress with small green dots and a black patent leather belt across her broad waist.

The man was slight, half the size of his wife. He had a full head of mostly gray hair, bushy eyebrows, a thin face and ears too large for his head. He walked with a slight stoop.

When they both sat down, the woman said, "I'm Maria." She reached over and grabbed her husband's hand. "This is Lenny. We're here about our son, Sebastian."

There was a knock on my door, the door opened and Downs came in. I asked her to pull up a chair. Downs slid a chair out from the conference table and sat down.

I said, "I wish I'd more information to share on your son's whereabouts, but we've only begun our investigation. We didn't know he was missing until this morning."

"Ms. Grant called me last night." Maria looked over at the nameplate on my desk. "Chief McCain?"

"I'm sorry. Yes, I'm Chief McCain, and this is Commander Leslie Downs. She heads up our investigations organization."

Maria said, "Ms. Grant told me if she hadn't heard from our son by this morning, she was going to report him missing. We packed immediately and came as quickly as we could schedule a flight from LaGuardia. When we arrived, I called Ms. Grant. She said that she'd met with you this morning. That you were going to investigate it."

Lenny asked, "What can you tell us?"

"Not much more than what Ms. Grant told you," I replied. "We found Sebastian's car at the place he was staying, along with his cellphones. Beyond that, we're trying to dig into whom he'd seen and talked to over the last few days. I'm hoping you can tell us more about him."

Maria began, "He's a good boy, Chief."

Before she'd finished the sentence, Lenny burst into tears. "Our boy has problems. We have tried to get him to move back home, to be with family, but we couldn't convince him."

"Problems?" Downs asked.

Maria said, "Sabastian suffers from ADHD, attention deficit/hyperactivity disorder. When he's on his medications, he does all right. He's smart, Chief McCain. Real smart."

"That disorder can affect people differently," Downs said. "How does it affect him?"

"You mean when he doesn't take his medications?" Maria asked.

"Yes."

"He has a violent temper. He has little or no patience. He has difficulty focusing. He can become fixated on things. He's impulsive, and he has violent mood swings. His doctor thinks that Sebastian may also be bipolar, but he's hesitant to make that diagnosis since the two disorders tend to overlap. When Sebastian's on his medications, he can function. But his condition requires regular visits to his doctor, which Sabastian is loath to do."

"Is his doctor is in New York?" Downs said.

Maria said, "He is, and he has a doctor here in Coronado Beach, too. Getting him to go is another matter."

"Is it a matter of money?" I asked.

Lenny offered, "Between insurance and our own resources, Sebastian's health care costs him nothing. It's not the money. I don't know what it is."

"He has a master's degree in criminology and was going to law school until he lost interest and dropped out," Maria explained. "When we got him back on his medications, he went through the police academy in Seminole County, and the City of Lake Mary hired him. He did well for two years, and then they abruptly fired him because his partner had beat up someone and framed Sebastian for it. He sued the department for wrongful termination, and the city settled with him rather than try the case in court. The city admitted that had they screened his medical history properly, they'd not have hired him in the first place. He received the equivalent of three years' pay, and that's when Sebastian's decline really began. That was when he took up with that woman."

"What woman was that?" Downs asked.

"Jane," Lenny said. "Before Lake Mary fired Sebastian, he responded to a domestic dispute. Jane Steel...no, Frost. Jane Frost and her husband were going through a divorce, and the PD dispatched Sebastian to their home to break up a fight. He helped her get a restraining order against her husband and started seeing her."

Maria chimed in, "Before Jane and her husband got a divorce, she was a health food nut and convinced Sebastian that the medications his doctors prescribed were poison. She was just as sick as Sebastian and had mental issues of her own. Once she got a divorce and a settlement, she sold her house in Lake Mary, moved to Coronado Beach and bought a house, and Sebastian moved in with her. That was five years ago. Their relationship was toxic and explosive. I'm no doctor, but I thought they both had an unhealthy dependence on each other."

Downs said, "You seem familiar with the details of your son's life. How is this possible with you in New York and your son here?"

"I spoke to my son every day," Lenny said. Tears streamed down his cheeks. "Every day, he'd call me. Sometimes it would be five minutes, and other days we'd talk for an hour. He called me Pop." More tears. "He never missed a day."

I addressed the next question to them both. "Your son described himself as a minimalist. Would you describe him that way?"

Lenny said, "Sebastian had odd views. He could be paranoid and cheap in the extreme. If we didn't provide him with a car, he wouldn't have one. Instead of trading in our vehicles, we would give them to Sebastian, and he'd run them into the ground. We'd leave the titles in our names, because he refused to put his name on anything or pay for insurance."

"Would Sebastian have any reason to disappear?" Downs asked.

Maria answered, "I don't think so. He's very territorial. We had to shame him into coming to see us every year or two, and then he'd only stay for two days at the most."

"Do you have any thoughts on who might want to harm your son?" I asked.

Lenny answered, "He would not talk about his business. Ever. So I can't speak to people he did business with. He had a violent and confrontational relationship with Jane Frost. Whether she's capable of harming Sebastian, I couldn't say. But she's the only person that comes to mind."

"Is there anything else you can think of that might help our investigation?" I asked.

"Yes. I'd like to offer a reward of ten thousand dollars for any information that leads to our son's whereabouts."

"I'd suggest that you contact the local newspapers and radio and television stations," Downs said. "When we leave the chief's office, I'll introduce you to our community affairs officer, John Hocking. He could help you with a press release and get you in touch with the right people." She stood up. "If you'll come with me, I'll make the introductions."

Maria and Lenny Sabatini stood up.

Maria said, "Thank you, Chief McCain. If we can be of any further help, let us know."

Firestorm

Lenny shook my hand, and Downs escorted the couple out of my office.

Downs returned in ten minutes. "I have interviews set up with Sabatini's ex-girlfriend, Jane Frost, and a neighbor named Taggart. They both live in Coronado Beach on beachside. Do you want to join or not?"

"I'm coming."

7

We took Downs' unmarked cruiser to beachside to a stucco home on a 1940s vintage Spanish-style block. A ten-year-old sun-faded Mazda Miata sat in the drive, with the top down and the seat backs tilted forward to shade the seat bottoms from the sun.

A woman with dark hair in her early forties answered the door wearing a two-piece bathing suit with a white cover-up that hung to her ankles cinched around her narrow waist. She was tall and wore her hair up in a ponytail. She led us through the the house that had Mexican tile on the floor, arched doorways and rattan furniture with bright red and blue cushions. We followed her to the back porch, which butted up to a small pool and a screen enclosure that covered both. A glass filled with ice and a bourbon-colored liquid sat on a glass-topped end table next to an open hardback book.

She gestured for us to sit on two chairs constructed of half wooden barrels with royal blue cushions.

The woman sat directly opposite Downs and swung her feet up on the chaise. While Frost was almost attractive, a scar on the left side of her face from just below her ear to the corner of her mouth left a deformed appearance. If it bothered her, nothing in her demeanor gave any evidence.

"I haven't seen Sebastian in six months. And if he's missing, I've no idea where he is."

I asked, "How did you know he was missing?"

Firestorm

"His parents called me yesterday. They wanted to know if I'd seen him. I don't know if I can be of help to you either."

"We were hoping you could shed some light on your relationship with him," Downs said.

"It is a short, ugly story. We had an intense relationship when it began, while it lasted, and when it ended." She reached for the glass on the table next to her chaise, took a sip and returned it to the table.

Downs asked, "Why did you break up with him?"

"He assaulted me. And he was a freeloader."

"When did he assault you?"

"When I told him that I didn't love him anymore." Frost swung her legs off the chaise, put her feet on the concrete deck and leaned forward with her hands in her lap. "This is a complicated story. He was complicated."

"We have time. Tell us about him."

She reached over to her drink and drained half the glass. "You are sure I can't get you something?"

"We're good," I said.

"I met Sebastian years ago. I was having a tough time with an abusive husband. My ex had punched me and slashed me across the face with a knife during an argument, and I called 911. My ex and I had squared off in the kitchen. I had grabbed a frypan off the stove and threatened him with it. Sebastian came to the house and broke up the fight."

"He was the police officer who responded to the call?" I asked.

"Yes. When Sebastian saw the cut on my face, he lost it and beat my ex, first with a punch in the face and then in the chest and stomach. He kept beating him until the second cop arrived and pulled Sebastian off him. They took my ex to jail and charged him with battery. Had Sebastian not shown up, my ex would have killed me. When they cuffed my ex and put him in the police car, I gave Sebastian a hug and thanked him for rescuing me. He hugged me back, and that's when it started. Then he took me to the hospital, where they stitched up my cheek." She turned her head to show us the scar.

"My ex filed a brutality complaint against Sebastian, and the other police officer testified against him. Sebastian lost his job over it. I felt horrible and responsible.

"I filed for divorce and began seeing Sebastian. My ex was a real estate developer, and I got the house and a nice settlement. When the divorce was final, I sold my house in Lake Mary, bought a house here on beachside, quit my job as a paralegal and moved to the coast. Sebastian couldn't get work with another police department, so we moved in together and lived off my divorce settlement. Everything was okay, until the money ran out." She reached over for her drink and drained the glass.

She continued, "While we were living off my settlement, neither of us was working. We were inseparable."

Downs asked, "Did he display any violence or anger during this period before the money ran out, as you say?"

"Sebastian has a temper, no question, but nothing I couldn't manage. That was until I had to go to work. Then everything began to unravel. While I knew Sebastian was possessive, I didn't know how jealous he was until I started working again."

"What did his jealousy look like?"

Firestorm

"He followed me and stalked me at work. I got a job working for an attorney in Daytona. When I'd get home at night, he'd interrogate me and accuse me of cheating on him. It was awful. It escalated. He'd show up at my work unannounced and make a scene. I nearly lost my job over it.

"Months earlier, Sebastian had gotten a license as a prlvate investigator. He was very secretive about his clients. If he made any money, he didn't tell me. When I started work, I asked him to help me make the mortgage payment and to share expenses. He refused. A month or so later, after his antics began to threaten my job, I told him I wanted him to move out. He lost it. He threw me down on the couch, ripped my blouse open and tried to rape me. I managed to get free and ran out of the house to a neighbor, and he followed me. He called the police, and when they arrived, Sebastian accused me of assaulting him and ripping my own blouse to frame him. It all happened so fast, I was speechless. If my neighbor, James Taggart, hadn't stuck up for me, they'd have carted me off to jail instead of Sebastian.

"After Sebastian's overnight stay in jail, full-scale war broke out. While he was in jail, I took all his things out of the house, put them on the porch and had James help me change the locks. While I was at work, Sebastian smashed the locks, put his things back in the house and refused to leave. The next day, the Sheriff's Department served me with a notice of hearing. Sebastian had filed for a restraining order against me, if you can believe it.

"I explained my situation to the lawyer I work for. With James' testimony and Sebastian's history of violence with Lake Mary Police Department, my attorney was able to convince the judge that I was the one in danger. The judge ordered Sebastian to leave my home and to have no contact with me. But that didn't stop him. He continued to stalk me and harass me. James finally convinced him to leave me alone."

Downs asked, "How did he do that?"

"You'll have to talk to him, but he took pictures of Sebastian breaking into my home and convinced me that I was in danger. So I called the police. About six months ago, he quit bothering me. I sold the house he and I shared and moved here. This is my boyfriend's place.""Do you have any idea where we could find Sebastian?"

"I'd suggest you check with his parents. He called his dad every day. They told me they've no idea where he is either. I certainly don't and don't want to know."

"Sounds to me like you have plenty of reason to harm Sebastian," Downs said.

Jane Frost's faced reddened. "Six months ago, I'd have done anything to get rid of Sebastian. I know he has problems. As I said, I haven't seen him in six months. I don't know what changed, but my problem with him went away."

"What about his clients?" I asked. "Could he have gotten sideways with one of them?"

"Chief, he never, ever discussed any of that with me. At first, I thought he didn't trust me. Toward the end, I came to believe it was about the money and not wanting to share his earnings with me. In the years I spent with Sebastian, he never contributed a dime of his own money. Not one dime. I knew he was making money. He had work. He was constantly getting calls and walked outside the house to take them. If he had money, he certainly kept it hidden."

"You know him as well as anyone. Why was he that way?" Downs asked.

"He was stingy in the extreme and paranoid. He thought the government was spying on us. He used to rail against the IRS and refused to file a tax return. He had no credit cards and refused to get anything other than pre-paid cellphones because he was convinced that big business and government were tracking him. When he did use his own money, which wasn't often, he paid cash."

"Do you have any idea who might have wanted to harm him?"

"Anyone he ever dealt with. I'm sorry, that was a flip answer. I've no idea, really. Sebastian was difficult. I don't know of anyone specifically."

"I'm just curious," I said. "If he was so difficult, why did you stay with him so long?"

"Sebastian could be...thoughtful, supportive and fun to be with. He was intelligent and protective. When I went through my divorce, he was what I needed, someone who made me feel I was important. What I learned too late about Sebastian was that I was his prisoner and that all I was to him was a meal ticket. He was a parasite, and if I was footing the bill, I was important to him. It was all about the money or more accurately his unwillingness to part with his."

"Do you have any idea where he might have gone?"

"I would have said to his parents in New York, but they're looking for him, too. So no, I've no idea where he might have gone. But wherever that is, I hope he stays there."

As we drove across town to meet with James Taggart, I asked Downs what she thought of Jane Frost.

"When we talked to Sabatini's parents, they told us that their son sued the city for wrongful termination and that the city paid him a settlement. Yet Frost never mentioned it. Assuming the city paid for legal fees, three years' pay would have been about sixty-five thousand dollars after they withheld taxes."

"You think he kept that from Frost?" I asked.

"It would fit with the picture I'm getting of him. Either that or he lied to his parents."

"The parents said Sabatini claimed that his partner framed him for beating Frost's ex-husband. That makes no sense since the ex would have testified that Sabatini was the one who beat him."

Downs said, "I'll call the chief at Lake Mary and check it out. I know him."

"Did you believe Frost's version of events?"

"I don't know enough to offer an opinion."

"Do you think she's capable of harming him?"

"I've no idea, Jed. She seems like she's telling it straight."

For the rest of the drive, I tried to take the measure of Sabatini. There was no question that he had mental health issues. The words that kept coming to mind as I reviewed the information that we'd collected so far were *sociopath* or *extreme narcissism*. Although his parents hadn't mentioned obsessive-compulsive personality disorder, the common thread so far from his two girlfriends and his parents was his hyper frugality, a common symptom of OCPD. None of the people close to him had described any of the other common symptoms of OCPD, like highly disciplined neatness and organization.

Downs pulled down a beachside side street off A1A, turning away from the ocean. The house was cottage-size, as were all the homes on this street. The neighborhood was an eclectic mixture of worn-down and remodeled homes from the mid-1950s.

James Taggart was sitting on a shallow porch, waiting for us, when we parked the cruiser on the street in front of his house.

Taggart was a well-nourished man in his late sixties or early seventies. He wore a white ball cap with "Titleist" embroidered on the front, a bright pink golf shirt, tan shorts and flip-flops. His time in the sun had tanned his face, arms and legs, but the skin below his ankles and feet were white, a golfer's tan.

Downs introduced us, and Taggart stood to shake our hands, and then led us through the front door to a small living room with four chairs facing each other. He offered us something to drink. We declined, and we all sat down. Beach scene pictures hung on the walls, and a ceiling fan spread the conditioned air around the room.

I said, "As Commander Downs told you on the phone, Sebastian Sabatini is missing. We understand you're acquainted with him. What you know about him might help us find him."

Taggart wore wire-rimmed glasses that sat crooked on his face. His blue eyes seemed bright compared to his darkly tanned skin.

"Sebastian is strange. Since Commander Downs called me and explained the reason for your visit, I've been trying to think of things that may be helpful to you in finding him, but I'm afraid I haven't produced much. It wouldn't surprise me if he just took off and faked his own disappearance."

"What makes you think that?" Downs asked.

"I don't have a good reason. It is just a feeling. How can I help you?"

"Tell us what you know about Sebastian."

"There are really three chapters to the story of Sebastian and Jane Frost and my involvement with them. There was the incidence of violence during the four or five years they lived together before she threw him out. Then he took up residence in the shed next door for about six months to harass and stalk her. After the city forced him to move out of the shed and off the property, he continued to stalk and harass Jane. My involvement ended about six months ago, and I haven't seen or talked to him since. Where should I begin?"

"Start at the beginning," I said.

"They lived in the house two doors down." He pointed toward the ocean. "They moved in about four or five years ago. Until she forced him to move out, they'd have frequent, violent arguments. Jane never raised her voice. Sebastian was violent. I could hear him screaming at her two doors away. When the arguments were loud, I'd walk outside. Often, Sebastian would fly out of the house, slam the door, yell obscenities at her from the yard, get into his car, rev the engine and roar out of the drive, burning rubber halfway down the block. I called the police multiple times, fearing for Jane's safety. Sebastian threatened me to mind my own business and to stay out of theirs."

Downs asked, "Did he ever get violent or assault you?"

"No. But he assaulted her when she asked him to move out."

Firestorm

"Ms. Frost mentioned that to us. She said that when she asked Sabatini to move out, he tried to rape her. She said she ran from the house to yours."

"I'll never forget that. I was sitting here, watching a golf tournament on television, and I heard her yelling for me. It was more like screaming. I ran outside, and Jane was hysterical. Her blouse was torn open, and she was crying uncontrollably. Just as she was gaining her composure, Sebastian came out of their house, holding a cellphone in the air, screaming, 'I called the police, you bitch. That's the last time you'll assault me again.' And he kept racing toward the two of us until I felt threatened. I told him to back away, that I wanted him off my property. He was seething, calling Jane every foul word he could think of. When he wouldn't back up off my property, with him standing in front of me, I called the police and demanded that someone come. When I did that, Sebastian moved to the street in front of my house, yelling obscenities at Jane.

"Before the police came, Jane explained that she'd demanded that he move out. He'd refused. Then he'd pushed her down onto the couch, ripped her blouse open and tried to pull her pants down. She'd managed to push him off and run out of the house. There was no doubt who was telling the truth. Sabastian had terrorized her.

"When the police came, Sebastian demanded that they arrest Jane for assault, but he failed to produce any marks or bruises to confirm his story. The cops kept Sebastian on the street, interviewed him and then interviewed Jane separately. I told the officers that I'd seen Sebastian's violent outbursts before and that there was no doubt in my mind he'd assaulted Jane, as she'd stated. They took Sebastian to jail pending charges. While he was in jail, Jane took all his belongings out of the house and put them on the front porch. I helped her change all the locks. They released Sebastian the next day because Jane wouldn't press charges against him. Jane was at work when he came to her house and found his belongings on the porch and the locks changed. I could hear him smashing the lock on the front door, and he put his things back into her house and refused to leave. When Jane got home, he wouldn't let her in. She spent the night with her sister in Longwood. The next day, the court served Jane with a notice of hearing. Sebastian had filed for a restraining order against her, if you can believe it. He intended to throw her out of her own house.

"At the hearing, with my testimony and the help of her attorney, the judge denied his request for a restraining order, ordered Sebastian out of the house and ordered him to have no contact with Jane."

Downs asked, "Why didn't she press charges?"

"Jane isn't the brightest candle on the cake. She didn't want anything bad to happen to him. She just wanted him to move out. She should have pitched the guy long before that. That's when he began living in the shed."

"Tell us more about that," I said.

"The house next door, the one between Jane and me, was vacant. An elderly woman, Gloria Aldridge from New Jersey, owns the house but hasn't been here for seven years. Sebastian looked after things for Gloria on occasion, and, when the court ordered him out of Jane's house, he called Gloria to get her permission to put his things into a large shed she had in her back yard. He didn't tell Gloria he had started living out of his car he'd parked in her yard and that he had eventually taken up residence in the shed. Gloria had turned off all the utilities on the property a couple of years before, so there was no running water, electricity or a usable bathroom, a very unsanitary situation. When I called the police about it, Sebastian told them he had Gloria's permission to be there. They called Gloria, who vouched for Sebastian. She told me later that it broke her heart that Sebastian was homeless and wanted to help him. The police refused to do anything because it was a code enforcement problem, not a criminal issue."

"Why were you so concerned about it?" Downs asked.

"Aside from all the sanitary issues of someone living in a shed next door to me, it was clear that his intent was to harass Jane. Even though Sebastian was under a no contact order, he'd break into Jane's house and use her shower and washer and dryer while she was at work and leave hate-filled, taunting notes in her bathroom and bedroom. When he was 'home,' parked in the back yard next to the shed, he'd scream obscenities over the fence at her and threaten her."

"Did she call the police?"

"No. I'll never understand that. I urged her many times to do something. I was concerned that he might hurt her. She'd defend him; she'd tell me that he hadn't harmed her.

"After six months of Sebastian's drama, I told him that if he didn't move off the property, I'd take whatever action I needed to take. I filed a complaint with code enforcement and convinced my elderly neighbor that her continued sanction of his living on her property was putting Jane's life in danger. Gloria called Sebastian and told him he needed to move, and he did, but he continued to harass Jane.

"For months, he surveilled her house, rifled through her mailbox, watched her at work and continued to break into her house when she wasn't there. I'd see him parked in the alley behind her house, or down the street making no attempt at stealth. Even then, Jane wouldn't report him to the police. Finally, I started taking pictures of him going into her house, confronted him and told him if he didn't stop harassing Jane, I'd turn the pictures over to the police. He dared me to do it. He said Jane would never file a complaint against him. I met with Jane and told her of my meeting with Sebastian and my threat to go to the police. I showed her the pictures of him breaking into her house, and she finally agreed to file a complaint with the police. Sebastian backed down. From the time the judge ordered Sebastian to leave her home, it was ten months before he relented."

"And he lived in the shed for a year?" Downs asked.

"No, six months or so. As soon as Sebastian stopped harassing Jane, she put the house up for sale and moved in with her new boyfriend, and things here returned to normal."

"When was the last time you saw Sabatini?"

"Six months ago."

Downs asked, "It seems to me you took Jane Frost's burden on yourself. Why?"

"What he was doing to her wasn't right. If something had happened to her, and I had had the power to stop it, I'd have felt horrible."

"Do you believe Jane Frost had anything to do with Sabatini's disappearance?"

"No. Despite the way Sebastian treated Jane, Jane loved him. I don't think she'd admit that, but there's no other explanation for her unwillingness to press charges against him for his violent behavior."

"Did Sabatini ever retaliate against you for your actions against him?"

"I didn't like Sebastian, but I treated him with respect. I met him for coffee twice and tried to reason with him. I explained that his obsessive behavior with Jane wasn't healthy and that the only one he was hurting was himself. I told him that it would be better for him to move on rather than involve the police, but he continued to harass her. After Jane filed her complaint, he abruptly stopped pursuing her."

"And that was six or seven months ago?" I asked.

"Yes."

"Do you know of anyone else that may have wanted to harm him?"

"Sebastian's persona was like a continuous, destructive, violent thunderstorm. He was intelligent and quite a salesperson when he wanted something. But if you confronted him or crossed him in any way, he'd do anything to destroy you."

Downs said, "You confronted him. Why didn't he come after you?"

"I don't know. He saw me as a father figure. He knew I wasn't afraid of him."

"He did threaten you," I pointed out.

"Yes, but he never followed it up with anything."

"Aside from Sabatini assaulting Ms. Frost, were you aware of any other times when he physically harmed her?"

"No."

Downs asked, "When Ms. Frost came to your house after the attempted rape, was there any indication Sabatini had hit her or physically assaulted her?"

"Not that I could see. But there was no question in my mind that he'd forcibly tried to have sex with her."

Back in the cruiser, on the way to the PD, Downs said, "I wonder why Jane Frost didn't mention Sabatini living in the shed next door after she threw him out."

"That was bizarre. Just when you think you've seen it all. I don't know what to think of it, except that it seems to track with him living in a camper the size of a small bathroom. I don't understand that either. What do you make of Frost's reluctance to press charges?"

"I've dealt with battered women since I joined the force. I can't tell you how often a man beats the living shit out of his spouse and she won't press charges, makes excuses for her husband and defends him. All the while, her face looks like raw hamburger. There's no question he was mentally and physically abusive to her. I don't get it. Maybe it's the battered-woman-syndome.

"You may be right. When she described why they broke up, she talked in terms of his unwillingness to contribute to their living expenses, that he was a freeloader. That was the final straw for her, not the abuse. The allegations of rape didn't come until after she'd made up her mind to end the relationship. Despite the verbal and physical violence from Sabatini, the relationship seemed to work if Frost was paying all the bills. It seems Sabatini's desire to remain in the relationship with Frost was more than greed. He was the one who couldn't let go, not Frost."

"This is all very interesting, but none of it explains Sabatini's disappearance."

Firestorm

"Do you give any credence to Taggart's belief that Sabatini may have intentionally gone missing?" I asked.

"Sabatini seems like an off-the-grid type of guy, Jed. If he were paranoid enough, he could have staged his disappearance. He has no credit cards, no trackable cellphones, and as a former cop, if he wanted to disappear, he'd certainly know how to go about it."

"That's a possibility, but my gut tells me something happened to him. We need to cast a wider net. Have your folks contacted the county and surrounding cities. Let's get a sheet on him, but I want to know how often Sabatini has come up on police radar. Check with the clerk of court for the county. Find out how many legal cases Sabatini's involved in and with whom. Also, Carl Stanton mentioned a retired Orlando Police Department cop on beachside who complained about Sabatini to police. See if you can arrange an interview. And we should put out a BOLO on Sabatini."

Downs said, "I sent a missing person report out on the wire earlier today. I must tell you, Jed, I'm not sure I want to find this guy."

"Leslie, we don't get to pick the cases. We work what's put in front of us."

"Well, there's nothing that says I have to be enthusiastic about it."

When we returned to the PD, I asked Downs to call the PD in Lake Mary to get background on Sabatini. Ten minutes later, she was in my office.

Downs said, "I spoke with the chief in Lake Mary. He said that they knew Sabatini's charges that his partner framed him for the assault were bogus. The chief said they had the testimony of Frost's ex-husband to prove it. He said that if it had been up to him, he'd have taken the suit to court, but the city attorney wanted the case 'to disappear,' in his words. They settled with Sabatini for seventy thousand dollars, or three years' pay, to make the case and Sabatini go away. The chief said the attorneys were more concerned about public airing of the PDs dirty linen than a settlement."

"Did you ask him whether Sabatini had a history of violence while on the force?"

"He told me they had three other complaints and that he'd been written up and warned over one of them."

I asked, "Where did all that money go? It's obvious that he wasn't spending it."

"I think it is amazing that he just made stuff up and he was rewarded for it."

"It doesn't seem right that the victim suffers and the perp gets rewarded," I said. "And let me know when the crime lab gets finished going through Sabatini's car and trailer."

8

My relationship with Ashley Rand has evolved with caution. First, she was a prominent lawyer in Coronado Beach who had recently divorced Eddy Rand, her law partner. When they'd practiced law together, Eddy had focused on criminal cases, while Ashley had concentrated on general law. When they'd divorced, they'd divided the practice, severing all business ties. Eddy had kept the criminal side of the practice, while Ashley had retained the general law clients. Ashley despised representing criminal clients. When she and Eddy had been in practice together, when the need arose, she had taken on criminal cases and excelled. Once she had split away and started her own firm, she had stopped accepting criminal clients, referring them to Eddy. Her older clients who ran afoul of the law had insisted she represent them instead of Eddy. That had created a conflict of interest. There had been two criminal cases this year where Ashley had had to refuse to represent a client because Leslie Downs and I had been the lead investigators on the cases. While we continued to see one another, I knew that the potential conflicts concerned her and could constrain our relationship.

Then there was Nicole, Ashley and Eddy's fourteen-year-old daughter. While Ashley had introduced her to me, she kept Nicole at arm's length, and for good reason. Nicole had been eleven when Eddy announced that he was gay and that he'd a hidden relationship with one of the officers of the Coronado Beach Police Department. The coming-out, the divorce, the custody hearings and the establishment of separate households had traumatized Nicole, and Ashley was reluctant to introduce the complications of a new suitor into the mix.

Ashley and I dated only on nights Nicole stayed with her father. Ashley permitted me to come by her home only when Nicole wasn't there. I supported Ashley on these precautions. Until we were confident in the direction of our relationship, these restrictions were practical, though it dampened spontaneity and the development of our relationship. It was worth it. Ashley was intelligent, beautiful and sexy. She was successful and well respected in the community, and wanted to be with the likes of me. After Sarah James' death, I wasn't in a hurry to make commitments either, so the growth in our relationship, albeit slow and plodding, suited both of us.

I was surprised when Ashley accepted my invitation to dinner at my house, which included Nicole. I'd extended similar invitations to her and Nicole to go out to dinner in the past, though not to my home. She'd thank me and tell me it was too soon. I'd made a habit of including Nicole at first to be polite, then after out of habit. When she finally accepted, I was both shocked and panicked when she agreed to include Nicole.

Ashley had been to my house before and been unimpressed. While I'd worked hard to get grass growing in the yard, shrubs clipped into shape, and the outside of the house repaired and painted, Ashley and AJ were constantly on my case to do a major renovation. It was all in fun, of course. Both her home and mine were on the Indian River. Her house fronted the river, while mine backed onto it. Her house was a vintage restored mini mansion. Mine, built in the 1950s, was as large as her living room, single story and of cookie-cutter design. When you stood in the street facing my house, it looked like a storage shed for AJ's house next door, something AJ reminded me of frequently. He'd say, "Young man, I'll lend you the money myself if you'll please do something with that house." Or, when he and Ashley ganged up on me, he'd say, "Boy, you have a million-dollar lot and a thirty-thousand-dollar house." Between Ashley and AJ, the ribbing was unabated.

With Nicole and Ashley coming that evening, I had a one-man GI party on the inside of the house. It smelled of disinfectant and glass cleaner, and while none of the furniture matched, it was clean. I'd purchased a picnic table for the small patio between the rear of the house and the dock. The T-shaped dock was the nicest feature of the house. I scheduled the cookout for seven, with dinner at eight.

When the doorbell rang at six forty-five and I opened the door, I fully expecting to see Ashley and Nicole, but Ashley stood alone. I looked beyond her to her car.

"Nicole will be coming in a half hour or so. She had a soccer game tonight. Eddy will drop her off after she stops by the house to clean up."

Ashley wore white cut-off jean shorts, a sleeveless royal blue blouse that hung outside her shorts, and her long black hair in a braid that hung over her left shoulder. Her makeup was spare and her skin darkly tanned. She stepped inside, wrapped her arm around my neck and kissed me. She carried a small Publix Supermarket bag, with the top of a bottle of wine exposed in her other arm.

"Nicole is excited about coming over," she said, walking past me into the kitchen, where she set the wine on the counter. Her gaze was everywhere, examining the living room and then the kitchen/dining room combination. She walked to the sliding glass door that led to the patio and looked out at the river and the dock.

"I can see why you like the dock, Jed," she said, picking the only nice thing about my place to comment on and ignoring the rest. This was Ashley's way of taking a shot at me over my aged and dated house. While she's been to my house several times, we went through this charade each time.

I recalled the first time Ashley had seen the inside of my house. When she'd come through the front door, there had been an unmistakable look of disbelief on her face.

She had wended her way through the kitchen/dining room, the small master bedroom and bath, then the other two bedrooms and hall bath. The bathrooms had pink and black tile, the windows were all jalousie type, the floor was terrazzo, and all the walls were white plaster. Ceiling fans whirled in every room, and newly installed central air conditioning had a tough time cooling the house, with air escaping through the ill-sealing windows.

"Interesting," she'd said breezily as she passed me and aimed back toward the kitchen.

I'd laughed.

"What're you laughing at?" she'd asked, a wide smile stretching across her thin face.

"You hate it."

"Hate is such a strong word."

"Is there anything you like?"

Firestorm

"I'd kill for this lot. Such a beautiful spot. I have to walk across Riverside Drive to get to my dock and the water. You have it right out your back door. With the back of your house facing west, your view of the sunset is spectacular."

That was months ago.

Ashley walked outside and looked out at the river.

"I just got the picnic table the other day," I said. "I figured we'd eat al fresco and enjoy the sunset."

"Nicole loves hamburgers. She'd eat them for every meal if I let her."

"I'm not much of a cook, but I can cook a mean burger."

"Let's have a glass of wine and go sit on the dock until Nicole gets here."

I got two wine glasses from the stained plywood cabinets in the kitchen, opened the bottle of Chardonnay that Ashley had brought, snagged ice out of the freezer and poured two glasses to near the rim.

Ashley followed me out the slider, over the small concrete patio, up the step to the dock, then out to the end where the dock teed. We stood taking in the view of Riverside Park on the other side of the river.

"This is impressive, Jed. It is the best view on the river."

"Yeah. I spend a lot of time out here." I pointed to two of the three folding chairs I'd just purchased for tonight. We pulled the chairs close to the built-in bench, sat down and put our wine glasses on the bench. "The breeze on the river is always nice this late in the day. I love being out here."

"Did Katherine Grant come to see you? She works in my office."

"Yes, early this morning. We've been working the case all day. Interesting fellow, this Sabatini."

"He's a piece of work, I'll give you that." She took a sip of her wine. A sailboat under engine power glided past, the captain and passenger waving. We waved back. "Sebastian did work for us for a while. He was a decent investigator. Eddy used him on criminal cases, but occasionally I'd use him in divorce cases, or when I represented an insurance company, I'd employ him from time to time on fraudulent claims cases."

"You said Sabatini 'did' work for you. Why did you stop using him? Was it his temper?"

"Oh, he had a temper, but that isn't the issue I had with him. It was the tactics he used to get information, or the way he harassed people when he felt they were hiding things from him. He had a very heavy hand, Jed. I was getting too many complaints."

"Do you think Eddy might have any idea where Sabatini might be?"

"I've no idea. You should ask him. It's been months since he did any work for me. I've no idea what Katherine sees in him. When he came to the office, which was seldom, he looked and smelled like last week's laundry. He was intense, too. That's what I remember most about him, intense and intimidating. Eddy could manage him. I couldn't. Sebastian showed me none of the respect that he showed Eddy."

I took a sip of wine and changed the subject. "I'm pleased Nicole is coming tonight."

Apparently sensing the real question behind my statement, she said, "It's time." She reached over and put her hand on mine. "I feel good about us and where we are. Besides, Nicole was beginning to feel like I was hiding something from her."

Firestorm

"What do I say to her? What do I talk to her about?"

"Nicole isn't shy in the least, Jed. Finding something to talk about is the least of your worries. Getting a word in...now, that's a challenge. She's constantly asking me about you and the police department."

Behind us, I heard "Lee," Eddy's nickname for Ashley.

We turned in our seats to see Eddy and Nicole Rand coming around the side of the house. We got up from our chairs and walked back down the dock to meet them.

Eddy was athletically lean, in his late thirties, with short graying hair. I'd met him several times over the past nine months and had never seen him in anything but expensive suits. Today, he had on a white T-shirt, denim shorts and flip-flops. Nicole wore denim shorts, an untucked white blouse and running shoes with no socks.

He said while walking toward the dock, "We tried the front door, then figured you were out here."

As Eddy stepped up onto the dock, I said, "Good to see you, Eddy," and shook his hand.

When I turned toward Nicole, her resemblance to her mother struck me.

Nicole stuck her hand out. "Hi, Mr. McCain. It's nice to see you again."

Nicole wore her long black hair down and examined me with her mother's gray eyes. She looked and had the demeanor of a girl in her late teens.

I said, "If you call me mister again, I'll arrest you for something. Just call me Jed."

She giggled. "All right."

"Well, my work is done," Eddy said. "I'll leave y'all to this gorgeous evening."

"Eddy, could I have a quick word?" I asked.

Leaving Nicole and Ashley, Eddy and I walked out to the end of the dock and sat down.

"What's up?" he asked.

"Sebastian Sabatini is missing. I was wondering if you've any idea where he might be. I understand that he did work for you on occasion."

"Katherine Grant talked to me yesterday and asked me the same question. I haven't seen Sebastian in three or four weeks. I have no idea where he is. I have no idea where he lives."

"Where did you last see him?"

"He came to the office about a month ago to pick up payment for work he did for me."

"What kind of work?"

"All of it was client confidential, so I have no details for you. I'm a defense attorney, so all the work had to do with criminal cases."

"Can you think of anyone who might want to harm him?"

"I don't think so. All his work was behind the scenes in support of my clients. He was helping them, so I can't imagine any of them wanting to harm him."

"Was he paid well for what he did?" I asked.

"Very."

"Cash?"

"Yes. I had a moral struggle paying him under the table. He insisted, and he was good at what he did, so I consented."

"Do you have any thoughts on who might have abducted him?"

Firestorm

"Sebastian was a hard case, Jed. He could take a deep breath and make someone angry. I put up with his shenanigans because he got results. But he'd come in dead last in a personality contest."

"Can you think of anyone who might know of his whereabouts?" I asked.

"Other than Katherine, no. He was self-contained, Jed. A loner. That's all I really have for you."

"Do you know of anyone else he did work for?"

"No. It never came up, and it would have been inappropriate for me to ask."

"Thanks, Eddy." I shook his hand, and he disappeared around the house.

Ashley and Nicole joined me at the end of the dock. Ashley was right, Nicole dominated the conversation, grilling me about the police department, what I did, what it was like to be chief. She wanted to know how many murders I'd investigated in New York and why I'd wanted to retire from such an exciting job. I'd look at Ashley's face and her obvious pride as Nicole conducted an in-depth interview.

An hour flew by, the sun bled out, and I had to interrupt Nicole so I could grill the burgers before the light disappeared. She had her mother's charm and personality. She and I hit it off instantly. I thought about Ashley's statement that she liked where we were. I had to acknowledge that. It had been more than three years since Sarah James' death, and I allowed myself to enjoy my relationship with Ashley without guilt.

Ashley left to return Nicole to Eddy's house. While I waited for her to return, I thought about Nicole holding court on the dock, peeling back my layers like someone might peel away the petals of a flower. If I'd had any reservations about committing to a relationship with Ashley, they disappeared that evening. Little did I know how fragile that relationship really was.

9

Sergeant Cory Cox of the Coronado Beach Police Department parked his personal vehicle in the shadows down the street from the American Legion Hall off Canal Street. He grabbed a nightstick off the passenger seat, then ambled through the small parking lot until he found the black Dodge Challenger he sought. He crept to the rear of the vehicle, scanned the empty parking lot, and, when satisfied he was alone, he smashed in the driver's side taillight. After inspecting the lot again to see if the noise had raised anyone's attention, he backtracked out of the parking lot, got into his car and left.

Cox had surveilled his target for more than a week. He knew the man spent most evenings at the Legion Hall and left routinely after it closed at ten o'clock. The man would drive the same route home every evening: east on Canal Street, north on US 1, left on Eleanor Avenue and then onward to his home.

10

Ashley returned to my house about nine-thirty. She'd changed her clothes, and it was obvious from the low-cut top and skimpy skirt that she had more on her mind than talking about Nicole.

We walked out to the end of the dock, and she said, "You made one hell of an impression on my daughter, Chief McCain. She talked about you all the way to Eddy's."

Although the sun had set, there were traces of purple on the horizon to the west, even at this late hour. The gnats and no-see-ums, prevalent at dusk, were gone, and a strong breeze out of the west was warm but comfortable.

"She's amazing," I said. "She has your good looks and personality. Her confidence in herself was so impressive."

"She always asks me about our relationship. She just doesn't want to know, she wants details. On the way over to Eddy's, she asked me if we were having sex. I nearly ran into the back of the car in front of me—that kind of detail."

"What did you tell her?"

"I tried to deflect the question, but she persisted, and I told her the truth. Then she asked me why you only come to our house when she's at Eddy's."

"I want to hear the answer to that question."

Ashley reached over and put her hand on mine. "I told her that I didn't want her to think that anyone could replace her father, and that I didn't want her to feel I was forcing a new man on her. Then she surprised me. She told me she knew that her father's announcement that he was gay really hurt me and that I'd every right to be angry and upset about it. She said that I had a right to be happy and to find someone else. She said she was happy when I began dating and wanted to be a part of it. She said she'd forgiven her father but hoped I'd find someone that made me happy."

"That shows maturity, Ashley."

"Then she asked me how often we had sex, and I told her it was none of her business."

We both laughed.

11

It was ten o'clock, closing time for the Legion Hall. Cox parked his CBPD cruiser in an empty parking lot on US 1 and waited. The Challenger went past him, headed north, at ten-fifteen.

The white light from the gaping hole in the taillight was clearly visible. Cox pulled out of the lot behind his target and closed the gap between them. When the Challenger turned to the west on Eleanor Avenue, Cox flipped on his lights and pulled the car over near a vacant building just before the railroad tracks. He'd picked this site because there were no homes nearby and the street would be empty at this time of night. He checked the license number on his laptop for wants and warrants to make a recording that he'd followed procedure, and then he flipped on the spotlight and aimed it at the driver's side door. He keyed the mic to the outside speaker.

"Get out of your car, please."

A tall, heavyset Black man slid out of the seat and stood in front of his open door. Cox exited the cruiser and stood in front of the grille.

"What's this about?" the man asked as he squinted against the bright headlights and spotlight.

"You have a broken taillight." Cox moved between the man and dashcam in the cruiser and began yelling, "Get your hand out of your pocket. Get your hand out of your pocket." Then Cox drew his service weapon and shot the man twice in the middle of the chest. With his body still blocking the dashcam, he advanced toward the man, who had collapsed on the ground, bent over him, placed the man's right hand into his pants pocket and rolled the man over onto his stomach. He stood up, keyed the shoulder-mic on his belt radio, reported an officer in need of assistance and requested an ambulance.

While he waited for help to arrive, Cox considered whether he should have used a throwdown weapon and placed it in the man's hands as he'd done half a dozen times before. He dismissed the strategy. The only weapon he had access to was one from a case the PD had assigned him to. It would have been too easy to trace it back to him. He'd thought about trying to buy one on the street, but again, it would leave a loose end. He decided simple was better. The department might discipline him for mistakenly shooting someone, or he might lose his job, but convicting a police officer of murder or even manslaughter was rare. He'd take his chances. Better to lose his job than spend the rest of his life in prison.

12

It was nearly ten-thirty when dispatch called me and said the words that no chief of police wants to hear: "officer-involved shooting."

I asked, "Is the officer okay?"

"Yes, but the person the officer shot is dead at the scene. And Chief? It's a Black man."

"Who was the officer?"

"Cory Cox."

"Any other officers at the scene?"

"I called Commander Downs. She's secured the scene and asked me to notify you. There are also other officers who responded to Cox's call for assistance."

The dispatcher gave me the address. I hung up.

Ashley sat up in bed. "Did I hear right? Cory Cox?"

"That's what she said."

"That's Eddy's ex-boyfriend."

I said, "I know."

"Is he okay? Eddy will be devastated."

"He's okay. He shot someone, though. I don't have any other details."

Ashley said, "I need to call Eddy."

On the way to the scene, my mind raced. When the dispatcher had said a Black man had been killed, the name of Trayvon Martin, the young unarmed Black male George Zimmerman had shot and killed in Sanford, Florida, in 2012, came to mind. A jury had acquitted Zimmerman, but the Sanford City Manager

Firestorm

had fired the chief of police after a no-confidence vote by the city commission for the chief's handling of the investigation. The outcry and demonstrations by the Black community had struck a nerve in the psyche of the nation, and the City of Sanford had become ground zero for their anger. Martin's name had become synonymous with police brutality, even though Zimmerman was not a police officer.

What had angered the Black community was that the police department hadn't immediately charged Zimmerman, and they felt that the department didn't take the loss of a Black life seriously. From the ashes of the lost life of Trayvon Martin and the riots In Ferguson, Missouri, over the death of Michael Brown at the hands of a White police officer, the Black Lives Matter movement had been born. That had encouraged the formation of other local groups who'd leapt on every opportunity, legitimate or not, to accuse the PD of brutality. As I rushed with lights and siren to the scene, my mind went to the worst possible scenario: mobs roaming Canal Street, looting businesses and burning buildings to the ground.

Halfway to the scene, I called Jim Cahill.
"We have a situation, Jim."

"I know. Leslie Downs called me. I'm five minutes out."

"Good."

While a small percentage of Florida's sheriffs and cities used FDLE to investigate all officer-involved shootings, many didn't, preferring instead to use their own internal investigation organizations. Cahill had convinced me, since our department was so small, to refer all officer-involved shootings to them. When I had become chief, I had amended our standard operating procedures to bring in FDLE immediately should the occasion arise. Cahill argued that since the Night Fire serial killer case had marked my tenure with the department with controversy, it was better for my longevity as chief to allow the FDLE to take the blame for this investigation and any fallout from it. I agreed. As an inducement, Cahill assured me that any investigation done by his organization would involve me; they'd lead the investigation, but we'd provide support. Because of the Martin case, Cahill had conducted training at the PD with all officers and supervisors when the situation required them to use deadly force. Cahill used the Trayvon Martin and Michael Brown case studies on what to do and not to do.

Cahill said, "I asked Downs to freeze the crime scene until we arrive. I also instructed her to ensure that no one disturbs the site, including your officers."

"I trained Downs, Jim. She knows what to do."

"Do you have any details?"

"Only that Cox fatally shot a Black man."

I thought if Cox had shot a White man, the situation would be quite different. We'd investigate the shooting in the same way, but without the scrutiny that would surely come because the victim was Black. As a chief of police, with the inflammation of racial politics in our country, I prayed every night that the situation would not require any of our officers to take a life. To get a call that it was a Black man was a blow.

When I arrived at the scene, CBPD cruisers completely blocked Eleanor Avenue. A dozen or more police, fire and ambulance vehicles, all with lights flashing, crowded around the dead man lying on the asphalt. I wedged my unmarked car between a fire and rescue vehicle and Cox's cruiser. Downs met me as I exited the car.

"The paramedics pronounced the man dead when they arrived," she said. "Two shots center mass. I bagged Cox's hands and service weapon, taped off the scene and had Cox sit in his car until you got here."

"Shell casings?"

"Left them on the ground. I also called Lieutenant Torres. I know Cahill will probably want to use his own people, but since Torres and her team used to work for them, I thought it might save time."

"Did you find a gun?"

"Unless the man is lying on top of it, no, I haven't seen one. I didn't want to disturb the body until Cahill gets here."

"What's Cox's story?"

"He won't say a word until his lawyer gets here."

I walked to Cox's cruiser. The driver's side door was open, and Cox was sitting on the front seat with his legs out and his feet on the ground. He was in his late thirties and over six feet tall, and looked overweight with his bullet-proof vest on under his uniform shirt.

As I approached the car, Cox stood and acknowledged me with "Chief" and a nod of his head.

I asked him, "Can you tell me what happened?"

"On the advice of my attorney, I've been instructed not to answer any questions until he arrives."

"Sergeant, you know the drill. We need to know what happened."

"And I'll tell you, but not until my attorney is present."

"Just answer one question for me. Was the man you shot armed?"

He looked me straight in the eye but made no attempt to answer my question.

"I need you to go back to the station. I need you to fill out an action report on what took place tonight. FDLE will come to the PD after they're finished at the scene. If your attorney is coming, they should meet you there. I'll have Commander Downs arrange to have another officer drive you back to the station after our crime scene folks process you."

Cox nodded but said nothing.

Downs met me at Cox's cruiser. "Eddy Rand is at the crime scene line and wants to talk with Cox. He says he's Cox's attorney."

"Tell him to meet Cox at the station. After the techs test him for gunshot residue, I want you to have another officer take Cox back to the PD. They should wait in one of the interview rooms."

Downs said, "I called the ME. He's on the way. Torres just arrived and is standing by. I ordered all non-essential emergency vehicles away from the scene." Around us, drivers started engines, and PD cruisers, fire department vehicles and an ambulance looked like carnival bumper cars as they all jockeyed to back away from the scene.

Downs instructed Cox to follow her, and they left me standing next to Cox's cruiser. With the other vehicles leaving the scene, the only lights on the body were those of Cox's vehicle headlights and spotlight.

Just as Cahill and the M.E. van arrived, the first television truck parked as close to the scene as the crime scene tape would permit. I recognize John Knight from Channel 9 news. They were preparing for a stand-up. That was the last thing I wanted to deal with. It was just over an hour since the shooting had occurred, and the unidentified dead man still lay on the street. One of the departing paramedics had draped a sheet over the body.

Cahill looked uncharacteristically casual in shorts, a T-shirt and deck shoes without socks. "What do we have?"

I answered, "We have a dead man in the street, shot by one of our officers, who refuses to discuss what happened."

Downs, having handed Cox over to Alicia Torres for processing, returned.

"Let's have a look." Cahill led us to the body, bent down and pulled the sheet away. He looked up at me and then Downs. "Did anyone find a gun?"

Downs said, "I was waiting for you. I didn't want to disturb the body. I didn't see one. I'm hoping for Cox's sake we find it underneath the body."

"You called Torres, right?" Cahill asked.

"She's here waiting on you. She's with Cox now."

"I want to get pictures of the body before we move it. Tell her to bring gloves, too."

Downs moved away toward the crime scene van at the same time the M.E. found his way to the body.

Damon Hunter was sixtyish, tall and gaunt with hollow cheeks, sunken green eyes, and ears too large for his head. He said, "Got here as soon as I could, Jed. I don't move as fast as I used to."

After Torres cleaned Cox's hand of gunshot residue, Downs placed Cox in a patrol car and had one of the officers take him back to the PD.

Torres got a camera and gloves out of her van, and she and Downs returned to where the body still lay in the street. Torres acknowledged everyone and handed gloves to Cahill and me. Hunter was already wearing his.

Downs, Torres, Hunter, Cahill and I crouched next to the body.

Cahill said to Torres, "Let's gets some pictures before we turn the body over."

Torres snapped pictures from different angles, the light from the flash punctuating the gravity of the scene. She chalked an outline of the body on the pavement.

Torres backed away, and Hunter struggled to roll the heavy man over. Cahill reached in and helped. The body looked strange, with one hand shoved down into his pants pocket. The first thing I noticed was there was no gun. There were two holes in the center of the chest, and the shirt was soaked with blood.

Downs said, "The best info we have, Doc, is the shots were fired at ten-sixteen."

Hunter removed the victim's hand from his pocket and patted the pocket down from the outside. "No gun!" He patted down the other pocket. "Nothing. There's nothing in either pocket."

Hunter asked Cahill to help roll the body over again. He patted down the two back pockets of his trousers and pulled a thin wallet out from the right pocket. He handed the wallet to Torres. "No weapons." He looked at the back of the man's head. "Someone rolled the body over. From the injury on his head, he fell backward when shot. There's little doubt that the COD is the gunshots to his chest, one or both penetrating the heart. You need to see anything else, Cahill? You're managing the investigation, I assume."

"Yes."

Alicia Torres, standing behind us, offered, "Driver's license identifies the man as Dwayne Robinson. His home address is just two blocks from here. His DOB makes him thirty-six."

While the three of us hunched over Robinson, Downs said, "I'm sorry, sir. You can't be here. This is a crime scene."

"I know that," John Knight said. "That's why I'm here. I asked one of your officers to tell the person in charge that I wanted to interview them, but they ignored me."

Hunter, Cahill and I stood up.

Cahill said, "Mr. Knight, you know better. You'll move back to the tape line, or there will be no interview. Am I clear?"

"At least tell me what happened here," Knight insisted. "It looks like one of your officers shot a Black man. Is he dead?"

"Commander Downs, escort Mr. Knight back to the tape line, and if he protests, arrest him for interfering in an investigation."

Downs pushed Knight toward the perimeter, Knight craning his neck all the while to take in details from the scene.

I asked, "Jim, do you want to deal with him, or do you want me to have our communications people deal with him?"

"No, I'll deal with it. But we have a problem here, Jed." Turning toward Hunter, Cahill asked, "Any reason to keep the body here any longer? The last thing we need is pictures of the deceased lying in the street on the eleven o'clock news."

"No. I can finish up at the shop." Hunter signaled for his assistant, who already had a gurney in place. They quickly bagged the body, loaded it on to the stretcher and rolled Robinson into the ME's van.

Cahill directed Torres, "You have the scene. I want the dashcam video from the cruiser in the PD in ten minutes. I want to see it before I talk to...Cox. That's right, isn't it?"

"Cory Cox," I said.

"Jed, we need to talk," Cahill said, pulling me away from Cox's cruiser into the shadows. "How did Knight get here so quickly?" Before I could respond with my theory that he had a police scanner, he said, "It doesn't matter. Knight will be all over this. He'll miss the eleven o'clock news cycle, but this will be big news in the morning. That doesn't worry me as much as how the Black community is going to react. Unless Cox has a damn good explanation, this makes the Michael Brown case in Ferguson look tame by comparison."

Back at the PD, Cahill, Downs and I huddled around the conference table in my office as Downs plugged a flash drive into her laptop, queued it up and hit the play icon. The video began at the point Cox had pulled the vehicle over. The Dodge Challenger clearly had a broken taillight. The video showed both Cox and Robinson getting out of their cars. Then Cox moved between the camera and Robinson, and Cox began yelling for Robinson to get his hand out of his pocket. Then Cox abruptly pulled his service weapon. Cox could be seen discharging his weapon twice, but the only thing visible was the outline of Robinson falling to the ground. Then

Firestorm

Cox holstered his piece, rushed toward the man and bent over out of camera range to check the man for vitals. Then Cox stood up, reached for the radio mic attached to the epaulet on his shoulder and called it in.

I had placed bodycams in the PD's budget for the last two years, but the city manager had cut them due to the cost. I had been lucky to get dashcams for all our cruisers approved. If we'd had bodycam footage now, we'd have known exactly what had happened. When I had been in uniform in the NYPD, I'd hated bodycams at first. When ordered to wear them, I'd felt like senior leadership didn't trust us. That had all changed when a man accused me of brutality while intervening in a domestic dispute. The bodycam footage clearly showed that I hadn't assaulted the man and had managed the situation in textbook fashion.

"This gives us squat," Cahill said. "Why did he stand in front of the camera?"

"You don't think it was intentional, do you?" asked Downs.

I asked, "Why would he do something like that? Hell, that video could have saved his ass. It doesn't make sense."

"I want to play it again." Downs restarted the video. "When Robinson gets out of the car, his hands are down at his sides."

"We still have nothing," Cahill said. "When Cox steps in front of the camera, you can't see what Robinson is doing with his hands. His right hand was in his pocket at the scene."

I said, "He had nothing in his pocket. What could he have been reaching for?"

When I'd seen the footage, it had crossed my mind that when Cox knelt before the man's body, he could have put the dead man's hand in his pocket.

We looked at the video again without gleaning any additional information from it.

Cahill asked Downs, "Is the recording equipment set up in the interview room?"

"Yes. It's just a matter of turning things on. Cox and his attorney are in there now, waiting on us."

"Jed, you need to suspend Cox. No matter what he tells us, until we've thoroughly investigated this, he can't be on active duty."

At the NYPD, this had been standard operating procedure. I hated it. It sent the wrong message to the officer, that he was guilty until proven innocent—that the department sided with the criminal. Despite the unfairness, the public concern of bias and the perception that cops covered for each other was a reality that we needed to manage. With the heightened scrutiny of police use of deadly force toward African Americans, I understood that I had no choice; I'd suspend Cox until FDLE investigated.

Cory Cox and Eddy Rand sat on the far end of a six-foot table. Jim Cahill and I took seats on the other side.

I spoke first, informing Cox and Rand that I was recording our session. I announced the date and time, and introduced the participants.

"As is the case with all our officer-involved shootings, FDLE will conduct the internal investigation. With me is Special Agent in Charge Jim Cahill of the FDLE. Are there any questions?"

Firestorm

"Why is it necessary to have FDLE involved? This should be an internal matter for the police department," Rand said.

I explained why we used FDLE to maintain impartiality.

Cahill said, "When you consider the implications of what happened tonight, that a White police officer fatally shot an unarmed Black man, we're sitting on what could be an explosive and dangerous situation. Within hours, the press and others will be tearing into this investigation like ravenous dogs. If there's even a whiff of bias or a coverup, or a feeling this department is unfairly defending one of its own, whether true or not, we could end up with the situation like they had in Ferguson or Sanford."

Turning to Cox, Cahill said, "Tell us what happened tonight."

Cox looked sideways at Rand. Rand nodded. Cox began, "I pulled a black Dodge Challenger over for a broken taillight. When the person got out of his car, he was reaching into his pocket for a weapon. I warned him twice to take his hand out of his pocket. He didn't stop. I feared for my life. I pulled my weapon and shot him. That's it. It happened in a flash. I had no time to think."

"What happened after you shot him?" Cahill asked.

"I squatted down and felt his pulse. He was dead."

"Did you move the body?"

"Yes, I rolled him over."

"Why did you do that?"

Cox didn't say anything. He looked sideways at Rand again.

Cahill continued. "You were looking for a weapon?"

Cox again looked at Rand, who tilted his head toward Cahill.

"Yes," Cox said.

Cahill said, "He wasn't armed."

"No."

"What made you so sure he was reaching for a weapon?"

"His movement was aggressive. I just reacted. If he'd done what I asked him to do..."

"Did you see anything that would indicate he had a weapon in his pocket?"

"Like I said, it happened so fast. He was going for something in his pocket, and I ordered him to stop, twice. What else could I have done? What would you have done?"

"Have you filled out your action report?" I asked.

Rand answered, "Yes, he has. I want to look it over before we give it to you."

"Until we complete the investigation, I'm placing you on suspension," I said.

"With pay?" Rand asked.

"For now."

"What does that mean?" Cox asked.

"It means that you're on paid leave, unless the investigation turns up something to contradict your story."

"There's no story. Look at the dashcam. It will prove what I'm telling you."

Cahill said, "When the man got out of his car, you stood in front of your dashcam. It proves nothing."

"That can't be right. You're serious?"

Firestorm

"There's nothing on the cam footage to support your claim. All we see is you pulling your weapon."

"I yelled at him twice. You didn't see that?"

"Yes. Eventually the court will release that video to the public, and there's nothing on that video that proves he reached for anything, much less a weapon."

Rand asked, "Why would he make something like this up? It may be an unfortunate accident, but it certainly wasn't intentional. There are no grounds here for anything. I can show you case after case where officers have died because they hesitated when someone drew a weapon on them. Officer Cox did his job, and his reaction was textbook—according to his training. If anything comes of this, I can assure you that we intend to defend Officer Cox vigorously. And I warn you, if you bend to political pressure to penalize my client in any way, I'll sue the FDLE and the police department. Sergeant Cox is an exemplary officer who's served this department with distinction. Now, if there's nothing further, I think we're done here."

"We need to swab your cheek for DNA," Cahill said.

"Doesn't the Police Department already have a copy of that?" Rand asked.

"FDLE is conducting the investigation. We need a sample for our records."

"You haven't been listening to me, Agent Cahill. My client hasn't done anything to warrant an investigation. He did his job. You haven't established that a crime has been committed yet. I think we're getting the cart ahead of the ox. You'll need probable cause and a court order for that."

I said, "I'll need your badge, Sergeant Cox."

Cox undid the pin clasp, slid the badge off his uniform shirt and flipped it onto the table.

"As soon as we clear this up, I'll pin it to your shirt myself," I said.

13

When Cox and Rand departed the interview room, I turned off the recording equipment. It was nearing midnight.

I led Jim Cahill back to my office. I was surprised to find Leslie Downs camped out, waiting on us.

Downs stood as we walked in. "What did Cox say?"

Cahill said, "That he thought the guy was going for a gun, he feared for his life, and he shot him. He checked the body, and there wasn't a gun. He said he ordered Robinson not to put his hand in his pocket, and when he did, Cox shot him."

"Then he admits to making a mistake?" Downs asked.

"Not exactly," I said. "He blames what happened on the fact that the man failed to heed Cox's warnings. While he acknowledges Robinson didn't have a gun, he's not claiming responsibility either."

"The dash video neither proves nor disproves Cox's claim. It's inconclusive."

"This is the worst possible scenario," Cahill said. "Can you show us that video again?"

The flash drive with the video was still in the USB port of my computer. Downs turned the computer on, I keyed in my passcode, and she pulled the video up on the screen again. We all watched as the scene played out. I asked her to play it through three more times.

I said, "You can see as Robinson got out of the car, Cox shuffled from side to side like he was positioning himself to block the dashcam's view." Downs ran the video one more time in slow motion. "See, he's shifting his position. It was intentional."

Cahill said, "That's speculative, Jed. How could we prove that? The only way that would make sense is if Cox shot Robinson with premeditation. This looks like a routine traffic stop."

"We're going to have every news organization in the country crawling all over us. We must investigate every single angle to this. What I see in that video is a man trying to block the dashcam's view. Eventually, someone will sue us to see this video. And if I can see him blocking the cam, then others may conclude the same thing. Jim, it's your investigation, but we need to dig into Robinson and see if there's a connection between him and Cox."

"I'll look into Robinson," Downs offered.

Cahill said, "That can't happen, Commander Downs." He looked straight at me. "Jed, neither you nor your people can be directly involved in this investigation."

"We had a deal, Jim. In these cases, we'd assist in the investigation."

"And you will, but we will lead it, and when we need your assistance, I'll involve you. I'll put my people on Robinson and Cox and see if we can find a connection. Downs, if you want to partner with one of my investigators, I'm okay with that, but there can't be any question that this is an FDLE investigation. And as far as you're concerned, Jed, the only public role you'll play is to announce the Cox suspension."

Firestorm

Just after midnight, on my way home down the deserted streets of Coronado Beach, I called Downs. "Did I wake you?"

"No. I'm still at the PD, going through files we found in Sabatini's trailer."

"Cahill told you to cancel any investigation into Dwayne Robinson. I want you to dig up what you can on him. This is between you and me."

"That was next on my list. There's a lot at stake here. We've worked too hard to build up the reputation of the department to have it crumble because of Cox. I'll dig up what I can tonight before I leave and have it for you in the morning."

When I got home, Ashley had dressed and was waiting for me.

"Eddy just called me. He told me what happened. He's very distraught. He asked me to intervene. He thinks you were too heavy-handed in suspending Cox."

"Ashley, you know I can't have this conversation, in particular with your ex-husband involved."

"Jed, I've never seen him like this. He's so upset."

"What would you like me to do?"

"Can't you put him on vacation or desk duty? Must you suspend him? It looks like you have convicted him before the investigation even begins."

"I'll tell you this, and then I want you to promise we won't discuss this until we resolve the situation with Cox. Cox shot and killed an unarmed Black man. In my mind, the fallout from this could be far worse than the Trayvon Martin case, and soon protestors will fill the streets of our small town, people who'll be more than happy to share their anger. I have many things to consider here, one of which is the safety of Sergeant Cox and this community."

"Sounds to me like you're covering your ass, Jed. What about standing up for one of your own?"

Ashley's words stung and were unexpected. I was silent for a moment. I wanted to tell her of my suspicions that Cox had shot the man intentionally, but I was certain she'd share the information with Eddy Rand first thing in the morning. The long silence gave Ashley time to reflect.

"That was unfair, Jed. You're in a tough spot, I know, but Cox is a good man and a good officer. You need to consider him in this."

"Ashley, I appreciate what you're trying to do, but I've made my decision on this. I can't discuss the case with you. You need to trust me that it was the right call."

"What do I tell Eddy?"

"Tell him what I just told you. That I've made my decision."

"All right," she said, but I knew she was extremely unhappy with my answer. "I need to go. Eddy needs me."

Ashley grabbed her purse and left with no show of affection.

My cellphone rang. It was Cahill.

"Jed. I hope I didn't wake you."

"Just getting home."

"I don't like the way I left things at your office."

"Jim, stop worrying. I'm good. I understand."

"I'll keep you informed, I'll get your input and, at a high level, we'll work together. Do I need to smooth things over with Downs?"

"No, I'll take care of it."

"We're good?"

"Yes, but I'm worried about tomorrow. When word gets out, what will the backlash be?"

"I don't know, Jed. I'll call the Volusia County Shoriff and the surrounding police departments and give them a heads up that you may need their help. I already called the governor's office and alerted them that we may need the National Guard."

"You really think it could get that bad?"

"I hope not, but if the worst happens..."

"And you'll manage the press?"

"Tell everyone in your department that if they're approached, they should refer all questions to us."

When I got off the phone with Cahill, I called the city manager.

"Do you know what time it is?" Jarret demanded.

"We had an officer-involved shooting this evening. One of our officers shot an unarmed Black man."

"Someone must have died, or you wouldn't be calling me."

"The Black man—his name was Dwayne Robinson—died at the scene."

There was a long silence, then Jarret said, "SHHIIIT. Does the press know?"

"Yes. They don't know all the details, but Channel 9 was there with John Knight leading the charge."

More silence. "And you say Robinson was unarmed?"

"The officer claimed that Robinson was reaching into his pocket for a gun. The officer yelled to him twice not to put his hand in his pocket. When Robinson ignored him, the officer shot him twice in the chest."

"Who was the officer?"

"Sergeant Cory Cox. I suspended him pending FDLE's investigation, per our agreement."

More silence. I could hear the words he was thinking: *It's been one crisis after another since we hired you, McCain.* Instead, he said, "This isn't good, is it?"

"No. You're familiar with what happened in Sanford with the Trayvon Martin case?"

"You think this is that bad?"

"I don't know, but we should plan for the worst."

"Let's meet first thing in the morning. Is Cahill on board?"

"Yes. He told me they'd manage the press."

"I don't like that. We need to get ahead of this. It is our city that will take the brunt of this, not FDLE. Can you get him to meet with us in the morning?"

"I'll call him first thing. I'm sure this will make the morning TV news shows."

"Damn it," Jarret muttered. "Seven in the morning, Jed. We need to get ahead of this," he repeated, and then hung up.

I called AJ McFarland, filled him in and asked him to meet with Jarret and me and the rest of the staff in the morning.

I grabbed a beer out of the fridge, opened the sliding glass door, walked out to the end of the dock and parked it on the built-in bench. The sky was clear, but the stars were hard to see with the light of the community center across the river and streetlights along Riverside Drive and Canal Street. The breeze on the river and the air, still warm from the heat earlier in the day, were calming.

The adrenalin from the events of the evening were still pumping acid into my stomach, and the violence that protesters might visit on our small town playcd through my mind like a horror movie. My mind raced with things that I would need to address first thing in the morning, like securing the town from potential protestors or the violence that accompanied events like this. And what about Cory Cox? While he was on suspension, he may become a target of those who'd want to take justice into their own hands.

And the investigation itself. I trusted Jim Cahill, but would he and his people investigate this incident with the same quest for the truth I would, or would they try to spin it to avoid a public outcry and sell Cory Cox short?

I scanned the horizon, and the sky west of the city had a faint orange glow to it. At first, I thought it might be streetlamps on Highway 44 leaving town that cast an orange hue, but the pattern was too wide. Coronado Beach was in its third year of drought, and the fires that had ravaged large sections of land last year picked up again with the heat of summer. Even the high humidity was not enough to eradicate the fire danger. But that was someone else's worry. I had headaches of my own to consider.

14

I called Martha Johnson at six the next morning. I asked her to get one of the interview rooms ready for a meeting at seven-thirty. When I arrived at seven o'clock, she was arranging chairs and fussing over the room.

"You heard about the shooting?" I asked.

"Yes, and before the day is out, there won't be a person on the planet that hasn't heard about it."

"Any thoughts or words of wisdom?"

"A White officer shoots an unarmed Black man. I think we're in for a world of hurt."

"I hope you're wrong, Martha."

"If BLM, Antifa or the Blacks Against Police Brutality get ahold of this, they'll try to burn this town to the ground. You better start praying for a miracle."

"I want you to sit in on this meeting this morning."

By seven-thirty, Johnson, Cahill, Downs, Neil Jarret, Mayor AJ McFarland, Tom Morris and John Hocking were all seated around the conference table, drinking coffee and chattering about the Cox shooting.

I said, "When the news hits the wires this morning about Cox shooting an unarmed Robinson, the world is going to descend on Coronado Beach. I want Commander Morris to go over our plan to deal with it. But first, Commander Hocking, why don't you give us an update on the press."

Firestorm

Commander Community Affairs John Hocking said, "Channel 9 morning news is the first local television station to carry the Robinson story. As soon as the story hits the wire services, the major TV and cable news outlets will be preparing to come here. We have a day before the shit hits the fan."

Commander Tom Morris, head of operations, said, "One day is all we need. Thanks to guidance from FDLE, after the Trayvon Martin case, we've done extensive planning over the past few years should this happen to any law enforcement agency in Volusia County. We have plans in place to deal with this. With a word from Jed, we can have the town secured by the end of the day."

AJ McFarland said, "Our downtown area is so small, I don't see how we can protect it."

Morris said, "We will blockade all the streets between US 1 and the Indian River and from SR 44 to Washington Street. We will reserve Riverside Drive, in front of City Hall, for the press and their trucks and equipment. Riverside Park will be set aside for protesters. It is large enough to accommodate a thousand to fifteen hundred people. I will assign officers from the Sheriff's Department and all police departments in Volusia and Brevard counties to secure the barricades, keep peace in Riverside Park and patrol the city."

"If the town is barricaded, how will people who want to protest get to Riverside Park?" Jarret asked.

"Electronic signs on the major roads leading into town will direct protesters to park at the airport north of town, where shuttle buses will transport them to and from Riverside Park."

"This sounds similar to the way we prepare for special events downtown when we close off the streets," AJ said.

"Yes, except for the heavy police presence."

Martha Johnson said, "What about people who don't follow those instructions? What if they park outside the barricades and push their way through them?"

"We've established six check points around the perimeter where shuttle buses will pick people up and ferry them to Riverside Park. No one can get on any of the shuttles with firearms or other weapons. We will run everyone through a metal detector or physically search them."

"Sounds like we're going to war on Black people."

Morris said, defending the plan, "The riots and looting caught police in Ferguson and Minneapolis flat-footed. Overwhelmed and unprepared, they lost control. We've had time to plan for this. We have today to get ready for what's coming. We either try to control it, or it will control us."

"Is this a perfect plan? No," Cahill said. "Morris is right. We have today to get ready. Anyone have a better plan?"

There was silence around the table.

Martha Johnson said, "I don't think you've any idea how big this protest could be. BLM, Antifa and BAP have paid goons to stir up a crowd with the goal of doing as much damage as they can. The PD is ground zero. It is a symbol they'll try to destroy. Whatever you think we need to do to protect the city, I'd multiply it by ten."

I said, "AJ, what're your thoughts?"

101

Firestorm

"We need to protect our town and the people in it. This may not be a perfect plan, and it may not work, but we owe it to our citizens to give it our best. You have my support if that's your call."

"We really don't have a choice, do we?" Jarret said.

Cahill said, "I've been in touch with the governor's office, and they assure me that if we need the National Guard, they'll support us."

"The Guard has already been in touch this morning," Morris said. "They're on alert and preparing to respond as early as tomorrow morning if needed."

I said, "Tom, make it happen."

15

Steven Hiles, a heavy equipment operator for the Florida Forest Service, backed his John Deere 650J FireLine Plow off a flatbed trailer on a dirt road south of Highway 44 and west of Interstate 95. It was eight-thirty in the morning, and the air was acrid with smoke. The goal was to contain the drought-fed Hunting Camp Road wildfire. West winds had forced the blaze toward the interstate, and Hiles' job was to plow a fire line east of the inferno, rob it of fuel and cut off the fire.

His plan was to cut a swath parallel to the old fire road. From atop the bulldozer, he surveyed where to enter the woods that edged the Spruce Creek Swamp. To his right, about ten feet off the road, he noticed a mound of disturbed ground covered in white sugar sand. The mound was distinctly different from the surrounding ground that was covered with pine straw and fronds from cabbage palms. As a former Army Military Police officer during the Iraq War, the size and shape of the disturbed earth was all too familiar. While he couldn't be certain it was a human grave, he couldn't prove that it wasn't either. He pulled his cellphone out of his pants pocket and called 911. He gave the operator directions to the site, described the orientation of the disturbed ground in relation to his flatbed trailer, stabbed at the phone to turn in off, then moved into the woods twenty feet from the mound and began carving a nine-foot path through the forest.

Firestorm

The emergency 911 operator dispatched a Coronado Beach patrol officer to the site. Once the officer confirmed the mound looked like a grave, he taped off the scene and called Leslie Downs, who in turn called the medical examiner's office. Forty minutes after 911 had dispatched the call, Damon Hunter and Downs crouched next to the suspicious mound. Downs had brought a camera and shot pictures of the scene from every angle.

Downs said to the ME, "From the lack of debris, it looks pretty fresh."

The doctor yelled to his assistant to bring a shovel, then instructed the younger man to begin digging. "Start around the edges. Don't be too aggressive. If there's a body in there, I want it in one piece."

Downs took pictures as the ME's assistant began the painstaking process of removing the dirt.

It only took five or six shovelfuls before his assistant found resistance. He knelt, and with a gloved hand, he began to dig, brushing dirt away from what turned out to be black plastic. As he removed more dirt, it was clear someone had wrapped a body up in two contractor bags, one slipped over the head and the other over the feet, using a rope to secure the bags around the waist.

The ME's assistant took a Swiss Army knife out of his pocket, slit the bag lengthways from head to foot and began pulling apart the plastic. The stench wafting from the opening took Downs' breath, and the assistant jerked his head away from the bag. Once the initial plume of putrid air had dissipated, the assistant pulled the bag open to expose a male face with dark features, thick black hair and a medium build, whom Downs recognized immediately.

"This is the man we've been looking for, Sabatini. I recognize him from his pictures."

Hunter instructed his assistant to get a small tarp from the ME's van and lay it on the ground next to the grave. He asked the assistant and the patrol officer to lift the body up out of the hole and place it on the tarp. After the officer complained that he was going to get his shoes messed up, he grudgingly aided in the removal of the body.

Once they set the body down and spread open the plastic bags, Downs took note of the condition of the corpse. There was a gunshot entry wound in the forehead above the left eye, but the absence of blood indicated that the scene of the shooting had occurred somewhere else. It could have been nearby, or the killer could have transported the body to the site.

Downs noted a dozen or so significant bruises on Sabatini's face. She'd seen enough domestic disputes to recognize the bruising from punches to the face.

Downs said, "We need to scour the area to see if we can find where he was shot." She called Alicia Torres and asked her to bring her team to the wooded site.

Hunter said, "With the body in that black plastic and the ninety-degree heat we've had this past week, and the state of decomp, I'd say the time of death was three or four days ago, certainly no longer than a week."

"That's consistent with the missing person report. It has been three days since anyone saw him."

"I'll be able to give you a better TOD when I get the body back to the shop."

Firestorm

Hunter's assistant helped him rol the body onto its side. There was bruising on Sabatini's upper torso and arms consistent with a beating. There were no other bullet wounds.

Downs took a dozen pictures of the body before the assistant brought a black body bag from the van and opened it up next to the corpse, and he and the patrol officer lifted Sabatini by the shoulders and feet, placed him in the ME's bag and zipped it up. They left the construction bags on the ground.

Downs said, "Maybe Torres can lift some prints off that plastic."

"As soon as I have something, I'll call." Hunter and his assistant got into the van, K-turned on the narrow dirt road and aimed back toward Highway 44.

Alone at the scene, Downs thought the smoke from the fire had thickened since she had arrived. She could hear the bulldozer in the distance and the crackling of small trees torn apart by the heavy equipment. While waiting on Torres and her team to arrive, Downs walked toward the tractor and flatbed trailer thirty feet from the gravesite. The driver had parked the rig on the grave side of the trail with the rear of the flatbed trailer facing her. Under the trailer, she saw a large stain in the white sand road. She walked around to the side and thought the stain could be blood. If it was blood, Torres could gather enough to test for DNA and match it to Sabatini. That would confirm whethor this was the primary scene of the murder.

Downs examined the lane to the front and rear of the heavy truck and trailer. While the road was little more than a dirt and sand trail, there was sufficient traffic to obliterate tire tracks. From the appearance of the tracks, all-terrain vehicles had made most of them.

Someone had fishtailed down the road, spraying sand from side to side.

Torres arrived with two of her techs.

"Alicia, that was the plastic bag we found the body wrapped in."

"We'll take care of it," Torres said, following Downs as she walked back to the flatbed.

Downs crouched and pointed to the dark stain on the road. "I don't know whether that's blood or not. If it is, we need to match it to Sabatini."

"I guess he's not a missing person anymore."

"Homicide, for sure." Downs pointed again toward the stain. "If that's blood, then the killer executed him there. Hopefully, we can find a shell casing."

"Can we get this truck moved?"

"With this fire, and the bulldozer cutting fire lines, I doubt it will be any time soon. Do the best you can."

"If he was shot on the road, I doubt we can reconstruct the scene."

"Again, do the best you can."

16

The crime scene was easy to spot as the gaggle of police vehicles and the Forest Service semi blocked the narrow white sand road. A smoky haze drifted across my windshield, and the air-conditioning system sucked in the acerbic smell and filled the car. What struck me as I approached was the isolation of the scene. Scraggly pine and cypress trees fought for survival with scrub palmetto in a low watershed now dry because of drought. There wasn't a house or any other structure in sight, the perfect place to dump a body.

Downs had called me about finding Sabatini. I parked behind the other vehicles and found Downs and Torres' crew conducting a grid search around the heavy truck. One of Torres' techs ran a special metal detector over the grassy area next to the flatbed.

I caught up with Downs. "What're we looking for?"

"A shell casing or anything else that shouldn't be out here."

I fell in beside her as she took small steps, inspecting the ground at her feet. "What did you find?"

"Single shot to the head. The killer buried him over there." She pointed to a hole surrounded by crime scene tape. "Doc says he's been dead for three or four days."

"You said the forestry guy found the body?"

"He found the grave. The M.E. dug up the body."

"What're the odds? If that ranger hadn't decided to park here, we'd have never found that body." I hated to admit how often dumb luck played a part in solving homicides. At the NYPD, the homicide clearance rate was around sixty-eight percent, just slightly above the national average. My own clearance rate was seventy-four percent, but luck had played a role in many of my cleared cases.

"We caught a break. Now let's hope it produces something."

"Could you tell anything about the entry wound?"

Downs said, "If I had to guess, I'd say the killer shot him with a .22 caliber handgun. I didn't see an exit wound when the M.E. pulled the body out of the hole. I hope the doc can recover the bullet."

Alicia Torres was fifteen feet away, moving debris around with her boots. I moved closer to her.

"Have you searched this area?" I pointed to the ground between us.

"Yep, you're fine," she said, still scanning the ground in front of her. She looked over at me. "You want to know what we found in Sabatini's camper and car."

I moved to within a couple of feet of her. She had her hair pulled up under a CBPD ball cap, and sweat was running down her face from the heat and humidity.

"How did you know that?"

"The only time you talk to me is when you want something," she said with a broad smile. Torres was an incorrigible flirt. While she had a Hispanic surname, she had bright green eyes, fair skin and a narrow face, and stood a foot shorter than me. My guess was she was of Irish descent, the freckles across the bridge of her nose and her cheeks prime evidence.

"We'll have to work on that."

Firestorm

"The file boxes we pulled out of the camper had Sabatini's prints all over them, as you'd expect. There were also traces of latex where someone had gone through them. You already know someone forced that camper door open, so it is safe to assume that whoever broke in used gloves to avoid leaving prints. That's all I can tell you about that. I have no idea on timing. The break-in could have been last week or months ago. If you asked me for an opinion, I'd say recent, but I can't prove that either. Downs has the files in the squad room. She went through them, so you'll have to speak with her about what her people found.

"About the car. We dusted it for prints. Sabatini's were the only ones we found. The two cheap cellphones in his car were pre-paid phones purchased from a big box store. We won't get much information from the cellphones, except the memory may have a record of recent calls. Sabatini's prints were the only prints on them. The car itself appeared as though he slept in it often. There were bed linens and a pillow, several changes of clothes, a towel and washcloth, soap and shampoo and other toiletries. Tools and a lot of useless junk filled the trunk. We went through all of it. Except for a hairbrush and toothbrush, which will have his DNA on them, there was nothing of consequence in the car or the trailer. Certainly nothing that would hint at his killer."

"Did you find any money in the camper?" I asked.

"No. We searched every square inch."

"And you didn't find any money in the car?"

"No."

"Everyone has secrets, Torres. We usually hide our secrets where we hide our money. Keep looking."

"Would you like to know some of my secrets?" She bit the end of her thumb and cut her eyes toward me.

"Torres, you have to quit doing that."

"That wouldn't be any fun." She laughed as I turned and moved back to Downs.

I said to Downs, "They can finish here. Walk out to the car with me. I want to hear what you found in the files from Sabatini's camper."

"I just gave the files a quick pass. I haven't had the time to do more. When I leave here, I'll go back to the PD and work on them."

"What about the tire tracks at the scene?" I asked.

"We took an impression of the tire treads on Katherine Grant's car, and they matched the unknown tread at the scene. The only tread unaccounted for is the one that matches our cruiser."

"When I met with Malcolm Hicks, his patrol car was a Ford Police Interceptor sedan like ours. The tire tread looks the same as those we found at the scene. Can you get a cast of his tires? It won't prove much, but it is a box we need to check."

Down said, "I'll take care of it."

"That is, of course, if we aren't needed for riot control," I said.

"Do you really think it could be that bad?"

"I don't know, Downs. We need to prepare for that event. If we're going to have a problem, it will be tomorrow night. What makes the Robinson case so difficult is that Cox shot the man intentionally, or at least that's what the dashcam footage tells me."

"Does this take priority over Sabatini?"

111

Firestorm

"Do you have an assigned role in Morris's plan to protect the city?"

"No. I'm subject to call, but this is primarily a mission of PD operations. If things get bad, we will need everyone."

"You have two priorities. Work the Sabatini case and do a deep dive on Dwayne Robinson. Robinson takes priority."

As I drove through town on my way back to the PD, I could see city workers assembling barricades and implementing Morris's plan.

17

On the way back to the PD, I called Cahill.

Cahill said, "FDLE is holding a press conference at the PD at two-thirty. Are you going to be there?"

"Yes. I'm on my way in. I'm just a few minutes away."

"Morris already has Riverside Drive blocked off, and officers were directing satellite trucks and press vehicles to park on the street in front of City Hall. Morris said that the Robinson shooting was all over the local morning news and that it would make the national news by the end of the day. Jed, local news had Robinson's name and that he was unarmed and Black."

"It doesn't surprise me," I said. "There were police, fire, rescue and private ambulance personnel at the scene. Any of them could have passed the information to the press. Charles Knight was there last night. He saw the body before the M.E. took it to the morgue. Who's doing the press conference?"

"I am. I want you to stand with me, but I want to make it clear that FDLE is conducting the investigation."

When I drove into the PD parking lot across the street from the Coronado Beach Marina, local TV transmission trucks from the four major networks lined the street. John Hocking, the community affairs officer, had already placed a lectern in the parking lot and directed the press where to set up cameras. It was still ninety minutes before the press conference, and from what I could see beyond the normal rubbernecking from passersby, there were no signs of protestors, violent or otherwise, gathering anywhere.

I walked up to Hocking and pulled him aside. "I thought FDLE was managing this presser."

Hocking said, "I called Cahill, and he said his people are on the way. They were coming from Orlando. The press started showing up around half an hour ago. Someone needed to deal with them. Before you go into the PD, the parents of Dwayne Robinson are in your office. They showed up minutes ago looking for answers on what happened to their son. I didn't figure you'd want them in the parking lot, available for interview by the press."

I wasn't prepared to talk to Robinson's parents. I believed that Cox had shot Robinson intentionally. The NYPD had trained us not to use deadly force unless we saw a weapon or our lives or the lives of others were in imminent danger. Seldom were threatening situations played out under ideal conditions. Frequently, they happened at night when an officer couldn't always see clearly what a perpetrator was doing. Or someone high on meth acted aggressively, turned toward an officer, and pulled something from his pocket after the officer had told him repeatedly to stop and put his hands on his head. When a police officer on the beat confronted a situation like this, there wasn't a committee of lawyers behind him, giving him advice on what to do. In a split second, situations forced officers to make life or death decisions.

Occasionally, the officer got it wrong. In my twenty-two-year career, I had had to make that split-second decision five times, the last a little over a year ago with the Night Fire Strangler. Although I'd never discharged my weapon on an unarmed person, I understood how, in the moment, one could make the wrong decision. You had so little time to think. Every time you took a life, you sacrificed a part of yourself. You couldn't erase it from memory. You'd always wonder if there might have been something you could have done to avoid the loss of a life. Justified as the action might have been, you'd grieve. I could only imagine how a conscientious officer who made the wrong call and took the life of another unnecessarily would be able to live with that for the rest of their life.

I'd aggressively defend an officer, ho, doing the best they knew how, made the wrong call and accidentally took an innocent life. When I'd looked at that video of Cox, there had been no question in my mind that he had been trying to position himself to block the view of the dashcam. With that on my mind, what could I say to Robinson's parents? How could I justify what had happened to their son?

As I was opening the door to the PD, I turned and saw Jim Cahill ambling across the parking lot.

"Hold up," he yelled to me.

I held the door until he made it past the threshold. "Robinson's parents are in my office."

"We should probably talk to them together," Cahill said.

"What're we going to tell them?"

"What we can. One of your officers shot their son during a routine traffic stop. We've suspended the officer pending an investigation. As soon as we've something more definitive, we will tell them."

"The fact that Cox shot an unarmed Robinson was all over the news this morning. Do we acknowledge that?"

"No. We don't deny it either. Unfortunately, Jed, this is going to end up in a lawsuit against the department and the city. You and I are going to have lawyers crawling all over us before this is over. We must be careful how we deal with this."

"His parents deserve to know the truth."

For the first time since I'd known Jim Cahill, he talked to me in the tone of a reprimand. "We don't know the truth. Until we know the truth, we offer nothing more than the bare facts. Are we straight on this?" He cut his eyes toward me. I'd never seen him this perturbed. "On the subject of the truth, the judge approved search warrants for Robinson's and Cox's vehicles and their homes. Since Cox refused to voluntarily provide a DNA sample, I also obtained a court order for that."

I asked, "Are you using our crime lab and techs?"

"Yes. They're all ex-FDLE and can give the case their highest priority. An extremely heavy workload has my crew in Orlando swamped. One of my agents will work with Lieutenant Torres."

"Can Downs be a part of your team?"

"Jed, I'd prefer she didn't. We've no idea what we're dealing with. This investigation must be independent."

"We had an agreement, Jim, that we'd assist with any investigations. What happened to that agreement?"

"Cox shot an unarmed Black man without cause. Unless we produce evidence to the contrary, it looks like Cox executed Robinson in cold blood. For what? A broken taillight? This is the worst-case scenario in officer-involved shootings. You need to stay as far away from this investigation as you can."

We stood on opposite sides of the hallway. I didn't say anything.

"I can't stop you from getting involved," he said, "but as your friend, I'm begging you to stand down and let us handle this. The alternative is for FDLE to back out and let you manage it. Do you want that?"

"No, but this is a stain on my department and my city, not yours. I'm not going to stand by and watch all that go up in flames. Yes, I'll trust you to manage it, but if I feel like I have to get involved, I will."

18

The Robinsons rose from the two chairs in front of my desk.

"Thank you for seeing us," Mr. Robinson said. "I'm John, and this is my wife, Laverne."

I introduced Jim Cahill. We all shook hands, and I directed the Robinsons to the conference table, where we could all sit comfortably.

The Robinsons were in their fifties and dressed as though they were going to church. They were both tall and lean, while their son had been tall, heavy and muscular. John Robinson was holding it together, but Laverne was on the verge of tears.

She said, "I've come to find out about my son." Tears streamed down her cheeks, and she gulped air trying to keep from losing it.

John Robinson put his arm around his wife. "We know that he's dead. We just want to know how this could have happened. How could someone shoot a veteran who's served his country dead in the street?"

Mrs. Robinson was now sobbing, her shoulders heaving as her husband tried to console her.

I started to speak, but Jim Cahill broke in and answered the Robinsons' question. "A Coronado Beach police officer pulled your son over for a routine traffic stop. During that stop, your son did something that made the officer feel threatened, so that he feared for his life."

Mr. Robinson asked, "What did he do that threatened your officer?"

"Our investigation is just beginning, sir. It will take time for us to piece together what happened."

"What did the officer tell you my son did?"

Cahill ignored the question. "The officer involved has been suspended pending the outcome of the investigation."

Mrs. Robinson sucked up her tears. "I saw on TV this morning that my boy didn't have a weapon. That you shot him dead, and he'd no way to defend himself."

"As I said, we're just beginning our investigation," Cahill said. "We don't have all the facts yet, and it is premature to discuss this case with you until we do."

I could see the anguish in the couple's eyes.

Cahill continued, "All we can do at this point is to offer our heartfelt sorrow at the loss of your son. I can assure you that we will do everything we can to find out what happened."

"You know, Chief McCain," Mr. Robinson said, "my son wasn't a saint, and he's had some issues with the law, but he certainly didn't deserve to be shot dead in the middle of the street, and certainly not for a traffic stop."

Mrs. Robinson added, "Our phone has been ringing off the hook since last night. Black folks from all around the country are telling us that this injustice will not stand." Her anger was building. "One of those groups called and said that you police would regret the day that you ever shot my boy. And I'm here to tell you, I hope they rip your asses apart." She stood up abruptly. "Let's go, John. They're just going to cover this over and blame it on the Black man. I hope they get what they got coming to them."

Firestorm

Laverne Robinson pulled her husband up by the arm and toward the door.

Mr. Robinson turned back to us and said, "This isn't good. I pray you're prepared for what's about to happen." His wife practically dragged him out of the office and out the front door of the PD.

In the hour between meeting with the Robinsons and the press conference, the scene had descended into controlled chaos. CBPD's officers and police officers from around the county and the Volusia County Sheriff's Department were busy barricading the city. By late afternoon, every person coming in and out of downtown would have to go through a checkpoint. Tomorrow morning, the shuttles would start to run around the perimeter and to the airport.

By the time the press conference began, we'd learned that Black Lives Matter and Blacks Against Police Brutality had both applied for and received a permit to hold demonstrations.

The press conference was short and to the point. Cahill read a brief statement:

"Last night, one of Coronado Beach Police Department's officers fatally shot Dwayne Robinson of Coronado Beach following a routine traffic stop. Since this is an officer-involved shooting, the Florida Department of Law Enforcement will investigate the incident. The police department suspended the officer pending the outcome of our review. Our investigation will be independent of Coronado Beach Police Department and will be fair and impartial. Since our investigation is just beginning, I can't discuss details of the case. As soon as we've concluded our investigation, I'll brief you on the results."

Cahill opened up the presser to questions.

"Was Robinson unarmed as has been reported?"

"What's the officer's name involved in the shooting?"

"What time did the shooting occur?"

Cahill answered these questions and many like it with "I'm sorry, I'm not at liberty to disclose that information at this time."

In the fifteen minutes set aside for questions, the only question he answered directly was how he spelled his name and his title with FDLE.

I followed Neil Jarret to his office in City Hall. He plopped down in his chair behind his desk with a *humph*. He said, "It's beginning to look like a military encampment. Already people are calling to complain that they can't get downtown because of the barricades. They're furious about the lockdown."

"I know John Hocking is working hard to get the word out."

"How bad could this get, Jed?"

"I don't know, but I think we need to warn the businesses downtown that they need to secure themselves."

"That doesn't give them much time."

"They have today and tomorrow. If we're going to have a problem, it will be tomorrow night. They have time."

"I'll take care of it."

I asked, "How are you handling this?"

Firestorm

"We have a serious problem," Jarret said. "Blacks Against Police Brutality are known to be violent and destructive. I know Cahill called the governor's office and asked the National Guard to stand by, but those resources won't be here before the morning. I don't think we've enough resources to hold off a mob if their intentions are violent."

"We've done extensive research and planning on this. We can control a thousand to fifteen hundred protesters in Riverside Park. That is if they remain peaceful."

"How did this happen, Jed?"

"Don't repeat this, but our officer murdered the victim. I can't prove it, and I don't know why he did it. But I intend to find out."

Jarret said, "That doesn't change the fact that people will blame you for what happened."

"Right now, that's the least of my worries. We need to find a way to defuse the potential for violence."

"How do you propose to do that?"

"We need to open a dialogue with the Black community today. When BLM and BAP roll into town, they'll try to enlist the local Black leaders to their cause."

"And if we can muster some support from them, maybe we can reduce some of the heat from the fire."

I said, "Exactly. I think we've worked extremely hard as a community to reduce racial inequality. We have regular meetings with Black leaders, and they've had significant input into our policing policies. Even though we've made considerable progress, the shooting of an unarmed Black man will be tough for them to swallow."

"Our first call is to Gabriel Banks. As a Black city council member, he's worked hard to reduce racial issues in our community. He'll not like hearing about the shooting."

"He'll like it a whole lot less if we have riots and looting," I said. "All his efforts and ours will have been worthless."

"I'll call him and ask him to meet with us as quickly as he can."

19

Back in my office, I spun my desk chair around and looked out the window. TV crews were folding up cameras and equipment they had used for the press conference in the PD parking lot and moved them to Riverside Drive in the front of City Hall. There, with City Hall and the PD in the background, TV correspondents set up their equipment for stand-up reports later in the day.

This wasn't the first time TV crews and reporters had filled our parking lot for a news conference. The city council had wanted to fire me when the Night Fire Strangler had brought national attention to our city; I didn't blame them. The serial killer had been part of my past with the NYPD and had come here seeking revenge. While I'd had no control over what the psychopath did and the murders he'd committed, I was the reason he'd come to Coronado Beach. If I hadn't been here, I'd have spared the city national scrutiny.

I'd survived because Cahill, AJ and Jarret had intervened on my behalf with city leaders. Without their raised voices, I'd be retired again and looking for another opportunity.

The Robinson shooting had the potential to plunge the city into the depths of extreme violence. As chief, I was accountable for what my officers did. The blame for what had happened rested squarely on my shoulders. The department, the city and its officials were collateral damage. AJ and Jarret were going to take heat for this, heat they didn't deserve. This time there might be nothing they could do to spare my job. In fact, their jobs might have been on the line as well. I didn't worry about me. My retirement from NYPD provided a good living. If the city fired me, it wouldn't look good on my resume, but I'd survive.

I didn't worry about AJ either. He was an elected official. It would take a special election to remove him from office before his term was over. AJ was well into his seventies and had accumulated considerable wealth before running for city council and then for mayor. He was set financially. He might bristle at the political fallout from the Robinson shooting, but he'd easily give up the office if he felt he could no longer be of service. And he'd told me that the only reason he had run for mayor was to help advance the goals of Neil Jarret and me.

I was concerned about Jarret. Still in his late forties, Jarret had a family to support and a long career ahead of him. The stain of losing his job during a racial event in Coronado Beach could hamper him finding other work. He'd have to move, and I knew he loved living here.

The firestorm Cox had created had resulted in the loss of two lives. I couldn't imagine what the Robinsons were going through as they mourned the loss of their son.

Alicia Torres and Leslie Downs appeared at my door. Torres wore a CBPD ballcap with a ponytail hanging out the opening in the back. Downs towered over Torres, and I was still trying to adjust to her red hair cut so short.

Downs asked, "Got a minute? Torres and I want to go over evidence that we collected from Sabatini's trailer and at the crime scene where we found Sabatini's body."

Firestorm

I waved them to the two chairs, and they sat down.

Downs said to Torres, "Why don't you go over what you have."

Torres said, "Let's begin with the trailer. As I told you, the only prints we found were Sabatini's, but we did find traces of latex on the boxes and files in the trailer. It has all the appearances of someone searching his trailer for something. Since there were files scattered all over, we think they were searching for a file. Whether they found it or not is unknown. We didn't examine the contents of the files. Leslie can report on that.

"We also found a strand of hair on one of the searched files that isn't a match for Sabatini. At this point, we don't know who the strand of hair belongs to, but it is being tested for DNA."

Torres flipped through her notes. "The burner phones. They weren't password protected. We were able to go back through call history on the devices and have an accounting of all the calls made from them. There was only one number that we could identify, and that number belongs to the Rand Law Firm. We can't identify the other numbers. All we know is that those numbers belong to other pre-paid phones. If we can find the phones, then the evidence might mean something.

"We have explained all the tire tracks at the scene of Sabatini's trailer except for one Leslie identified as a common tire on Ford Police Interceptor sedans. We took a molding of the tires on Sergeant Hicks' Sheriff's Department cruiser. They were a match. But, as Leslie has observed, it is a common tread found on many cars.

"We went through Sabatini's car and found nothing of any consequence. Everything we found in the car was consistent with someone living in it. We dusted it for prints, but the only prints that weren't his belonged to Katherine Grant. We found her prints on the car door, and they are consistent with her statement that when she arrived, she found the door wide open, and she closed it. Now let's go over the murder scene."

Downs set one file down and opened another. "Before we move to the crime scene, we found thirty-three files related to work Sabatini was doing for the Rand Law Firm. Twenty-nine were related to criminal cases and four divorce cases. There's no question that Sabatini made his money working for Rand."

Torres said, "At the murder scene, the M.E. reported that the time of death was within a twenty-four-hour window three days prior to us finding Sabatini's body. He said he couldn't be more specific because of the condition of the corpse. The killer placed the body in black plastic bags, in a shallow grave, in ninety-plus-degree heat, which accelerated decomposition.

"The M.E. said the cause of death was a gunshot wound to the head from a .22 caliber bullet. We examined the bullet in the lab, and the striations are clean. If we had the gun that fired it, we'd have no difficulty making a match.

"On the black plastic bag in which the killer wrapped the body, we found sweat and epithelial cells that we're testing for DNA. The samples are of excellent quality. If we have the DNA of the killer, we can make a match.

"The blood that we found on the sandy road was a match for Sabatini. There is little doubt it was the murder scene. The killer shot him on the road, dug a hole, then buried him.

"We also found extensive bruising on the face and torso, like he'd sustained a beating. I asked the M.E. whether the killer could have inflicted the bruising at the time of the shooting. He said the bruising on Sabatini's face and torso indicated that someone had beaten him a day or two before. Hunter told me that he found no evidence to connect the two."

I said, "Hicks told me he 'tuned Sabatini up' for threatening his friend Paula Cane."

"Tuning him up must have been one hell of a beating," Torres said. "I should have DNA results on the hair sample, sweat and epithelial tissue later today. The M.E. found marks on his wrists where someone handcuffed him."

"Leslie, bring in Sergeant Hicks. I want to hear what he has to say on the record."

"Do you want to know what I found out about Robinson?" Downs asked.

Torres said, "If you don't need me anymore, I have a full plate." She gathered her files, pushed her chair away from my desk and stood. Looking directly at me, she said, "if you want me, you know where to find me." Then she winked at me, smiled broadly, pushed the chair back toward my desk and left the office.

Downs said, "She's something else. But her work is exceptional."

"Yep, she's exceptional," I said.

Downs rolled her eyes. "On Dwayne Robinson, by reputation he's a professional button man and debt collector for loan sharks. He provides contract muscle to organized crime. He has a long history of assault and gun possession charges but only one conviction, where he served a two-year stretch for nearly beating a man to death. He's not a pillar of the community. Cox, however, has a spotless record. If there's a connection between Cox and Robinson, I can't imagine what it would be."

I said, "The fact that Cox deliberately positioned himself in front of that dashcam tells me there's a connection. Cox didn't shoot Robinson over a petty traffic violation."

"What do you want to do now? We are going to piss Cahill off if we dig around in his investigation."

"One of our own deliberately shot an unarmed man, and I want to know why. Keep digging."

"Jed, a background check on Robinson is one thing. Investigating Robinson and Cox on top of FDLE could jeopardize and compromise their case. Then where will we be? With all the scrutiny this case is getting, we must cross every T by the book. I don't know about you, but the last thing I want is to get sideways with Fiddle."

"You're right, of course. We will give it a day or two. If FDLE isn't making progress, then we will revisit this."

"Am I back on the Sabatini case?"

"Yes."

"I'll have Hicks in here first thing in the morning."

"Clear it with the sheriff."

Downs nodded and stood up. "Anything else?"

"You're a great officer, Downs. One of the best I've worked with."

"Thanks, McCain."

20

City council member Gabriel Banks had a formidable presence. He had a massive head and upper torso and stood well over six feet tall. He had a heavy white beard and balding head. His face was broad with wide cheeks and nose, his skin a dark shade of brown. His lips were large but expressive, and his smile disarming and contagious. In all my dealings with him, which were infrequent, I'd found him to be a kind, gentle soul.

I extended my hand to him as I entered Neil Jarret's office. "Pastor, it is so good to see you again."

His large hand dwarfed mine, and his handshake was firm. Even in his seventies, he carried himself like a professional athlete. His full-time job was pastor of the Coronado AME church.

We chose chairs around the conference table and sat down.

Banks jumped right in. "Mr. Jarret called me with some very disturbing news— news that came to me early today."

"Yes. Last night one of our officers shot and killed Dwayne Robinson. He was unarmed. Our officer claims that Robinson was reaching into his pocket for something after our officer instructed him to keep his hands out of his pockets. Our officer said he feared for his life and shot Robinson in the chest. We didn't find a gun on Robinson. Those are the facts. Right now, I have nothing more than that."

"Your choice of words, 'our officer claims,' sounds to me like you have doubts about his story." Banks' voice was deep and gravelly.

"Pastor, what I may or may not feel is irrelevant. The shooting occurred last night, and the investigation is underway. I don't have anything more to report than that."

"All right, then why am I here?"

"Our town is under siege with protestors from BLM and Blacks Against Police Brutality. These groups are busing people in from all over the state. If the history of Ferguson, Missouri, is any predictor of what could happen here, rioters could destroy our small town. I'm hoping that if we can open lines of communication with these groups, we can avoid this escalating into riots and looting."

"I ask the same question. Why and I here?"

"I'm hoping that the Black leaders of our community could influence these groups to voice their opinions peacefully."

"And you want me to spearhead that effort?"

"Yes." I looked across the conference table at Jarret, who had his fingers formed in a steeple in front of his lips.

Banks said, "BLM and BAP have no interest in justice for the man shot last night. They're interested in one thing and one thing only: political power. They use fear and intimidation to frighten people into adopting their racially divisive agenda. If you think I can meet with them to get them to play nice, you're kidding yourselves.

"I believe that this community, White and Black alike, have made a significant effort to eliminate racism in our community. And Chief McCain, in the three years you've been here, the tension between the police department and the Black community has lessened dramatically. None of this matters to them. They're interested in headlines and controlling the narrative. They're here to get those headlines through whatever means."

Jarret dropped his hands to the table and said, "Are you saying that there's nothing to be done?"

Banks stood up. "What I'm saying is, don't get your hopes up. One of your officers has shot an unarmed Black man. Regardless of the reason, it has the appearance of racism." He pushed his chair back up to the conference table.

I stood and said, "I assure you that all the resources of the PD and FDLE are working this shooting. We will find out what happened."

Banks said, "I believe you, but the people you'll be dealing with don't give a spit about justice. They're sharks looking for blood. I hope it doesn't come to it, young man, but they'll be looking for someone to blame. You're the most visible target. They'll want you to fry for this. That will be their headline."

Banks shook both of our hands. "I'll gather my fellow pastors and community leaders. I think we should meet with them as soon as possible. With their support, I'll approach BLM and BAP. I'm assuming that you'll both make yourselves available for a meeting if I can arrange it. The most that I can hope for is for you to get in front of these people, and you make your case. That's all I can do."

After Banks left, I asked Jarret what he thought about the meeting.

"I wish we had more time. Banks is a good man. He wants what's best for the community, but he's clearly upset by all this. He's trying to be gracious, but it puts him in a terrible position. What we're asking him to do goes way beyond his role on the council."

I said, "He's the only chance we have to head off what could be a dangerous situation. And I think he's the man for the job. He has the strength of personality, charisma and standing in the community."

While I was on my way back to my office, Ashley Rand called.

"We need to talk. I don't like the way things ended last night, and I'm missing you. I have a tough decision to make about Eddy, and I'm still his counsel. Until we settle this..."

"I understand, Ashley. Where do you want to talk?"

"Away from investigative eyes. How about the Outback in Daytona?"

"When?"

"Can you leave now?"

"On my way."

21

I'd met Ashley Rand on one of the rare occasions she was handling a criminal case. I'd wanted to question her client about his involvement in a murder. I'd wanted his statement, and Ashley had wanted legal assurances that we wouldn't pursue a murder charge in exchange for his testimony. She'd asked me to meet her for a drink to hash out the agreement. The chemistry had been immediate.

On my way to Daytona, I considered the difficult spot Ashley was in. I was investigating a case that involved her ex-husband and former law partner. We were in a relationship. Her involvement in Eddy Rand's discussions with us would be a complete conflict of interest for both of us. What she didn't know was we were preparing to bring her ex in for questioning regarding work Sebastian Sabatini had done for him.

Ashley was sitting in the lobby, waiting for me. She stood, and I kissed her and gave her a hug. She wore white shorts, a sleeveless black button-up blouse and white sandals. She had pulled her long black hair into a ponytail. Outback was notorious for noise, so we asked the host for a booth as far from the bar as possible. The host showed us to a booth in the back of the restaurant. We sat opposite each other.

"I have things I want to talk about that violate every ethical standard I'm supposed to follow," Ashley said. "And I'm going to trust that what I tell you will remain between you and me until the appropriate time. I trust you, Jed. And I'm going to put that trust to the test. Do I have your word?"

"Yes, of course."

"Eddy and I met today for lunch. Someone is extorting him to participate in an illegal scheme that bears directly on the Sabatini case. I'm not at liberty to discuss it further, but I can tell you that Sabatini is just the beginning. This is a much bigger case than that."

"What're you wanting me to do?"

"Let me finish. Based on what Eddy told me, I'm no longer representing him. He's hired his own counsel. He knows that your investigation will lead you to his law firm. He wants to get out in front of this."

"In front of what?"

"I can't tell you that. He's asked me not to. He wants to meet with you and Jim Cahill tomorrow."

"Why Cahill?"

"I can't tell you that either. He's insistent that we do it this way."

"When does he want to meet?" I asked.

"At his office at noon. He has a little legal work to do on his own behalf, and he needs time in the morning to do it."

"I'll be there and bring Cahill up to speed. I thought you weren't representing Eddy."

"I'm not," Ashley said. "What he has to say will be enormously helpful to your cases. He asked me to intercede in setting this up. He wants to avoid you escorting him in and out of an interview room. He wants to do this on his terms. I told Eddy that I'd help him with this but that he is on his own after that and I'll be free of it."

Firestorm

"I don't understand why you're so involved. You're no longer married to the guy, and you no longer practice law with him."

"I've one reason, and one reason only: Nicole. When we clean up this mess, I don't want Nicole to look at the man I love as the man who put her father in jail. I'm staying involved because I don't want anything to hurt her relationship with you. If our relationship is going anywhere, she must be a part of it. This is too important to me for Eddy to ruin it for me over his stupidity. I wish I could tell you more, but everything will become clear after your meeting with Eddy tomorrow."

The server came to take our order. Neither of us was hungry. She ordered a vodka martini, and I ordered a beer.

"Nicole really likes you, Jed. You've made such an impression on her. Eddy loves her, but before, during, and after the divorce, Eddy hasn't spent quality time with Nicole. She's at a stage in her development as a young woman where she needs the influence of a strong male figure in her life. When we came home from dinner at your house the other night, you were all she talked about."

"When you and I had that first drink at Outrigger's, and you asked me if I felt the chemistry between us? I did, and it was immediate and compelling. I felt the same way when I met Nicole for the first time. I don't want anything to set that back. But I can't make any promises about Eddy until I know the whole story."

We ordered appetizers and another drink, and talked about the Cox shooting. We discussed how BLM and BAP protesters had laid siege to Coronado Beach.

"What're you going to do?" she asked.

"The FDLE investigation into the Cox shooting will take its course. Everyone knows how important it is. With Cahill leading the investigation, I can't control that. But the politics of the shooting, that's another matter. Jarret and I met with Councilman Banks this afternoon, and he said he'll set up a meeting with the Black leaders of the community in the morning. I'm hoping that we've earned enough support from them over the past three years to enlist their help with BLM and other more militant groups."

"I know how hard you've worked building bridges there. With police officers partnering with leaders to reduce crime in their neighborhoods, you have earned their trust."

"Jarret has worked incredibly hard at finding solutions to poverty, education and finding jobs for the unemployed. Crime is down. People are noticing the difference."

Ashley said, "Maybe that will be enough."

"When a police officer shoots an unarmed Black man, it erodes that trust. The Cox shooting has created an ugly storm. The goodwill we earned will be hard to rebuild. I'm hopeful that we can meet with representatives of BLM and BAP and try to head off any reason for violence. The protests are a healthy way to deal with the angst of a racist act. It's the violence, looting and destruction of a riot that I fear. If these organizations are here to cause trouble, that would be the quick way to get national television and press coverage. That's what they'll want. We will need to find a way to remove that need."

"How can the Black leaders help?"

"I want to meet with BLM, BAP and any other group who intends to protest. I want our local Black leaders in that meeting who can and will testify to the work we have done to improve relationships with the community, Black and White alike. I want to assure them that the shooting of any unarmed person, regardless of color, by one of our officers is unacceptable, and we will vigorously and scrupulously investigate them."

"I've seen these people in action. They don't seem like people who're interested in any of that."

"It's worth a shot. It's either that or call in the National Guard."

"Given everything you've told me, the meeting with Eddy tomorrow is critically important."

"Well, you certainly have my attention."

Ashley said, "Speaking of attention, Nicole is at Eddy's tonight. Would you like to come to my house later?"

"Ashley, I can't. I need to spend time with AJ tonight. I need him to be at the meeting with the Black leaders in the morning, and I need to bring him up to speed. How about tomorrow night?"

"After tomorrow's meeting with Eddy, I don't know whether he'll be up to parenting. We'll have to see."

22

I called AJ from the car on my way home. When I arrived at the house, he was already sitting at the end of the dock, drinking a beer. When I approached, he held up a bottle wrapped in a New York Yankees koozie. "Bring me good news. I could use a little of that."

I took the beer, sat down next to him and said, "It's a beautiful night, isn't it?"

"I didn't mean that kind of good news." He pointed across the Indian River to Riverside Park, where a small knot of protesters had already begun their vigil.

"I think we're prepared for what's coming."

AJ took a swig of his beer. "What's coming, Jed?"

"I wish I knew. It's the unknown that makes me anxious. We can plan for what we think will happen, but what will happen is hard to predict."

"Do you think there could be rioting?"

"I think there's every possibility unless we do something to get ahead of this."

"That sounds optimistic. What do we need to do?"

"Jarret and I met with Councilman Banks this afternoon. We asked him for his help in defusing BLM and BAP. He agreed to pull together leaders in the Black community so that we could make our case. I'm hoping we can meet tomorrow—early. I think you should be there."

"I'm not sure what I can contribute."

Firestorm

"You can address all our efforts to put racism in the rearview mirror," I said. "You've worked hard for that, AJ. We all have. I'm hoping that Banks and the other leaders will echo that."

"Will any of that matter to them?"

"If it matters to our Black leaders and they lobby to prevent violence, I'm hoping that will be enough."

"I don't know, Jed. Yeah, we've made progress. While we may feel that we're succeeding, they may not share our assessment. There's still a level of mistrust there."

"I understand that. Enlisting their help is the only shot we have. If that doesn't work, I have no idea where all of this will lead."

"Did Banks say he'd help?"

"Yes, but nothing beyond putting this meeting together tomorrow. And to be honest, he didn't sound overly optimistic."

AJ drained his beer and said, "It's worth a try, I guess. At least we can say we made the effort." He stood up to leave. "An old man needs his beauty sleep. Let me know what time the meeting is, and I'll be there."

"I'll find out where from Jarret and call you."

23

As I walked into my office at seven-twenty, Sergeant Johnson was arranging chairs around the conference table.

"Did you see Riverside Park when you came in?" she asked. "The park is starting to fill up."

"No, but it doesn't surprise me. With the shooting hitting national news last night, I figured today would be challenging."

"The shuttle buses started running at six this morning. I know BLM is in the park because I could see one of their banners stretched between two palm trees. They aren't angry yet, but it's early. I'm worried. Folks in my neighborhood are upset about this. Very upset. I wouldn't be surprised to see their faces in Riverside Park today to express their outrage. This is bad, Chief. I'm worried about all of us."

I didn't respond. I didn't know how.

John Hocking, Lesley Downs, Martha Johnson, Jim Cahill, Neil Jarret and I found spots around the conference table. Tom Morris remained standing. He pulled his uniform belt up over his well-nourished belly. The red blotches on his boyish face were more prominent than usual. A tattoo of an American eagle adorned his left forearm, and his deep brown eyes showed concern that made me feel a little uncomfortable. I hoped that no one else noticed it.

"As of this meeting," Tom began, "we have fully implemented all our security plans. We've a full complement of officers from the Sheriff's Department and surrounding PDs, and we're as ready as we will ever be. Electronic signs on the way into town directing protesters to the airport appear to be working, and the shuttle buses as of six this morning began running between the airport and Riverside Park.

"We have completely blockaded the downtown area. We have police coverage around the barricades and at eight check points. Shuttle buses are making stops around the perimeter and depositing protesters at Riverside Park."

"What about residents and business owners?" I asked.

"They're all required to show ID to get in. Crowds at Riverside Park are small but mushrooming. BLM organizers have arrived and are setting up camp in the park. They aren't happy we put them in the park instead of in the street in front of City Hall, where we stationed the press. They don't like it, but they've accepted it. It doesn't appear that BAP is on-site yet. But they've filed for and received a permit. Tonight will be a real test. If there's trouble, it could begin tonight."

"What about the National Guard?" Jarret asked.

"We have two hundred guard personnel standing by in Deland and Edgewater. If asked, they can be in position within forty-five minutes."

Cahill said, "It looks like a war zone, but I guess we can't help it. We should protect ourselves."

"Yes, the city looks like a fort. But what else would you have us do?" Morris looked around my office for comments but received none. With all the confidence he could muster, he said, "We are ready. We developed a good plan, and now we work the plan."

I thanked Morris for all his hard work, then asked my staff if there was anything else to discuss. No one

142

spoke, so I dismissed the meeting. Jim Cahill remained. Everyone filed out. Johnson rolled her chair out of the office and closed the door behind her.

Cahill and I sat back down at the conference table.

Cahill pulled a file out of his backpack, set it on the table and flipped it open. He said, "I want to brief you on what we have on the Robinson shooting. Unfortunately, it isn't much.

"Robinson wasn't a pillar of the community, it appears. He had a long rap sheet. He called Raiford State Prison home for a stretch for aggravated assault after almost beating a man to death. He spends time at the American Legion Hall, even though the Marine Corp dishonorably discharged him for conduct unbecoming.

"We obtained warrants to search Robinson's home, car, bank accounts and credit cards. Torres has Robinson's prepaid cellphone from his car, and her techs are working to get beyond the passcode. Robinson had no checking, savings or any other financial accounts we could find. We did find a hefty sum of cash in his home. Given his background, we can only speculate that he did everything in cash.

"We also obtained similar warrants on Sergeant Cox. We didn't find anything of consequence except for a laptop. Cox had erased the hard drive. Torres' techs are working to restore whatever files they can. If there's a connection between Cox and Robinson, we haven't found it yet.

"We checked to see if Cox ever visited the American Legion. We showed his picture to vets who frequent the place, and no one recognized him. We've researched cases that Cox worked to see if he ever encountered Robinson in the line of duty. Nothing.

Firestorm

"We're still digging. We can't prove a connection. Not yet."

"Maybe we will find something on Cox's laptop," I said.

"I wouldn't get your hopes up. It's a long shot. It depends on how thorough he was in erasing it."

Neil Jarret let himself into my office. "Sorry to interrupt. Councilman Banks called me. We're going to meet with community leaders at ten in Council Chambers. There's enough room there for everyone to sit and gather around a table. I called AJ and asked him to be there." He backed out of my office and closed the door.

Cahill's report was disappointing news. I had been hoping we could go into the meeting with Black leaders with progress to report. Now I would have to go empty-handed.

I said to Cahill, "You should be in this meeting."

"What's this all about?"

"Jarret and I met with Councilman Banks and asked him to assemble leaders in the Black community to enlist their support with BLM and the other militant groups."

"Jed, I thought we agreed that you'd leave this investigation up to FDLE and let us manage all of this. We're supposed to be taking all the heat to protect you and your department. Now you're jumping right in the middle."

"I've let you oversee the investigation. But I'm not going to stand by and watch this town burn to the ground when I could have done something to prevent it. We need to defuse this situation before it gets out of control. What I'm trying to do may not work, but I'm going to try, with your support or without. I'd like you to be at this meeting. I want to convince these folks that we're serious about an impartial investigation. You can help."

Cahill was quiet for a moment and just stared at me. "This is a fool's errand, Jed. You might as well stick a target on your back."

"Will you help or not?"

"Yes, but I don't like it."

"We're good friends, Jim. That means something to me, but I must do this!"

"I understand. But you can't make commitments or promises to these folks on FDLE's behalf. That's the line you can't cross. If you do that, you'll put my job at risk."

Downs waited patiently for my brief sidebar with Cahill to end before knocking on my door and entering. "I have Sergeant Hicks in an interview room. Do you want to sit in?"

I nodded, stood up from the conference table and followed her to the interview room. Leslie had already set up recording and video equipment. She turned everything on, and we sat opposite Hicks. Downs announced the time and place and those in attendance.

Downs began her interview. "Sergeant Hicks, this interview is regarding evidence that we've collected concerning the death of Sabastian Sabatini. You have the right to have an attorney present, and you also have the right not to answer any of our questions. Do you understand that?"

"Are you going to charge me with anything?"

"No, not as this time. We talked with you informally, but now that we have a time of death and confirmation that you gave Sabatini a severe beating, we want to have your statement on the record."

"I've nothing to hide. I've told you everything. Yes, I gave him a beating, but I didn't kill Sabatini."

"We found tire marks matching your sheriff's cruiser outside of Sabatini's camper. You obviously had a motive; your beating of Sabatini substantiates your desire to repay him for the misery he caused Paula Cane."

Hicks asked, "When was the time of death?"

"Three days ago, between noon and five."

Hicks pulled a small black leather-bound notepad out of his gun belt. He flipped through the pages and handed it to Downs. "I was in Gainesville for a two-day continuing education seminar. The details are in here."

Downs recorded the details on her legal pad and handed the notepad back to Hicks.

"You were still only a couple of hours away," I said. "You had the time to murder him. Officers skip out on these classes all the time."

"Three other sergeants from the department went with me. We were in class together. Had meals together. Drank together." He gave us their names. "I hated that little bastard for what he did to Paula, but I didn't kill him. My alibi will clear me."

I asked him, "If you didn't kill him, do you have any idea who did?"

"No, I don't. But like I told you, Sabatini made it his business to make enemies. I don't know who did it. I just know it wasn't me."

"We will check your alibi. If it holds up, you won't be hearing from us again."

When Hicks left the room, I said to Downs, "The ME's report supports what he said. The beating happened a couple of days before someone murdered Sabatini. I never liked Hicks for this, but we should check all the boxes. Follow up on his alibi. Let me know if it doesn't check out."

"The Sabatini case has come to a halt," Downs said. "I have a boatload of nothing. We have evidence but nothing to match it to. What do you want me to do?"

"Check out Hicks's alibi, and then lend help to Tom Morris. He'll need it."

24

In my office, Cahill was sitting in my chair, talking on the telephone to one of his investigators. Behind the desk, dressed in an Italian-cut suit, he looked more the CEO of a corporation than a special agent for FDLE. Still on the phone, he stood and gestured for me to sit in my own chair, but I motioned for him to sit back down and took one of the guest chairs. The case he was talking about was unrelated to the Cox shooting. He said goodbye and got off the call.

It was five minutes before we'd walk over to City Hall to meet with the Black leaders.

"What do you want me to do at this meeting?" Cahill asked.

"I want you to assure these folks that every resource at FDLE is working this case. That you investigate all officer-involved shootings without partiality or loyalty to the police department. I don't need to tell you what to say. They need to know that we will not sweep anything under the rug."

"I can say that. I will say that. But I'll also say that we will recommend disciplinary action if we find you negligent in any way. We will say the chips will fall where they fall, regardless of who it hurts."

"Good. That's what you should say."

"What're you going to tell them?"

"I'll remind them of all the efforts both the PD and the community have undertaken to improve relationships. I'll remind them of how hard we've all worked. Then I want to get them to commit to defending this city against those who would want to harm it."

The council chamber had a long table used by attorneys during the council meetings. It was large enough to accommodate the nine of us milling about the room, making introductions and getting reacquainted. Councilman Banks had brought four other Black leaders, all pastors except for one man, Eddy Brown, who owned a furniture shop on Canal Street in the middle of downtown. He had run for city council in a different district than Banks two years ago and lost. Protecting his downtown business motivated him; he had real skin in the game.

I introduced Cahill to people I'd met and worked with for the past three years. They were good people.

When we all took our seats, mixed together rather than on opposite sides of the table, I drew encouragement from that. That didn't happen by design. It made me feel we were all in this together, trying to find a way through it.

Councilman Banks kicked off the meeting. "I met with City Manager Jarret and Chief McCain regarding the Robinson shooting. Anticipating the protests underway this morning, they asked me for our help in intervening with BLM and Blacks Against Police Brutality. Has anyone heard from either of these groups?"

Three other pastors raised their hands.

One of the pastors, dressed in tennis shorts and a white T-shirt, said, "They called and asked me to organize the members of my church to turn out for the protests. They threatened that if I didn't get involved, they'd go around me and canvass our neighborhoods."

149

Firestorm

The other two pastors said they'd received similar phone calls. No one had called Eddy Brown.

Banks said, "I have angry folks in my congregation over this." The other pastors nodded in agreement. "Robinson's criminal past and his involvement with organized crime are well known to us. The poor in our community fall victim to loan sharks and drug dealers who demand payment. Robinson is a pariah of the worst sort. But our officer shot Robinson in cold blood. There's nothing to justify that. Nothing. So, when I get calls from those trying to organize a response, I'm sympathetic. However, I know the violence that could come from this, and no one deserves that either. We didn't shoot Robinson, but we will all pay the price."

Banks looked directly at me. "Chief, I know you mean well, but there's nothing you can say to me or the Black folks gathering in Riverside Park that will change what happened. You could even charge Cox with murder, and it will not bring Robinson back to life. All they'll hear is that a White police officer shot an unarmed Black man."

AJ said, "Jed was hopeful that with your support, we might dissuade BLM and BAP from violence. I get that they're angry. I'm angry. All of us are. We didn't ask for this. It happened."

"There isn't anyone in this room without a stake in what happens today and tomorrow," I said. "We all…" I looked at each person sitting at the table. "We will all lose if this turns violent. If we can meet with BLM and it doesn't prevent a riot, so be it. But we need to try."

Banks said, "By meeting with them, there's a risk we could push them into a corner and make things worse."

"If we don't meet with them," Eddy Brown countered, "given what has happened in other cities, there's a high probability they'll riot. Doing nothing, or worse, giving them the appearance of our support because we don't oppose them, that's a recipe for disaster."

"What you all aren't seeing is this. If the Black leaders of Coronado Beach seem in opposition to these militant groups, it could anger them more."

"Pastor Banks, are you forgetting how we've all poured our souls into improving race relations in this city? These efforts were much more than words and politics. Every person in this room has made sacrifices and witnessed true change. Coronado Beach is a different town than it was three years ago, and we can all take credit. But Chief McCain has been the main driver. He's pushed all of us. Except for this unfortunate killing, policing in this city has changed. We can't forget that. If we can get a meeting with BLM and BAP and try to appeal to them, it is worth the risk."

Jim Cahill said, "I'd give you an update on the investigation, but that doesn't seem to matter at this point. I also feel that meeting with them could fan the flames, but there's a strong likelihood they'll riot regardless. With that in mind, if we meet with them, they might tell us what they intend to do. It would give us more information than we have now."

"I'll try to arrange a meeting for early this afternoon," Banks said. "Don't get your hopes up. They may not want to meet with us."

Eddy Brown said, "We have to try."

AJ stayed behind and chatted with Banks. The Black pastors left, and Eddy Brown remained.

151

Firestorm

While Cahill and I were getting up from the table, I asked Brown if the businesses along Canal Street had taken security precautions.

"How can anyone adequately prepare for something like this?" he replied. "In my own case, there isn't enough time to remove all the furniture and appliances from my store. I've an accurate inventory of my stock. I've removed all my records and files from the store, and I have good insurance. It's like preparing for a hurricane, only with less time to prepare. I have my employees boarding up the store. The rest is in God's hands. But there are other businesses in town that run on a shoestring. If there's rioting and looting, they'll not fare so well."

"I appreciate your words of support in the meeting," I said.

"You've earned them. I hope for all our sakes we can reason with these militants. I'll see you later, if Banks can put a meeting together." He reached out, shook my hand and left.

Cahill said, "This is a Hail Mary, Jed."

"Many a game has been won with a Hail Mary."

Cahill and I walked across the parking lot to the PD. As I tapped in the security code to access the back entrance, my cellphone rang. It was Ashley Rand, reminding me of our meeting with Eddy Rand in his office at noon.

25

When Jim Cahill and I arrived at Eddy Rand's second-story office on Canal Street, Ashley, dressed in a beige business suit, met us at the door and ushered us into Eddy's office.

She said to me, "Thank you for doing this." And she left Cahill and me alone.

The office looked as though the staff at *Southern Living* magazine had decorated it. Framed pictures of waterfowl hung on walls covered in light gray grass cloth. A couch, end tables and a love seat occupied a corner of the spacious office, and a conference table and chairs sat in another corner. A massive desk with four guest chairs consumed the other half of the office. All the furnishings were white wicker accented with dark gray cushions. Glass covered the end tables, conference table and desktop. Two white ceiling fans whirled quietly in the room that was large enough for a small group to make themselves at home.

Eddy Rand swept into the room dressed like he'd just stepped off the golf course, in white slacks and a royal blue golf shirt. His face showed little emotion. He shook hands with Cahill, then me, and joined us at the conference table.

"Before I begin," he said, "I want agreement that this conversation is off the record. I've gotten myself involved in something that bears directly on the investigations into both Sabatini and Cox. What I'll tell you will advance both of your investigations significantly. Initially, I was unknowingly involved in a criminal conspiracy that Cox used to blackmail me. Because of the potential of you charging me with a crime, I can't share with you what I know without incriminating myself.

"With the potential for violence, time is of the essence. What I want is complete immunity for my part In all of this. Cox coerced and extorted me."

Cahill said, "I'm sure you know I don't have the authority to agree to that. Only the assistant state's attorney can. And how can I plead for immunity if I don't know what you're going to tell us?"

"Here is what I propose. Our conversation will be off the record. I'll ask you to sign an agreement that you can't use what I share today against me and that unless I'm immunized from prosecution, I'll not testify to any of the information I'm about to disclose."

Cahill said, "I can't do that either."

"The ASA can authorize it. Given the seriousness of the situation you face, the situation we all face, you need what I know to bring these cases to a swift conclusion."

Eddy handed us a one-page agreement documenting what he was asking us to sign. He turned to the keyboard of his desktop computer and began typing. "I just sent an email to the ASA with a copy of what I'm asking you to sign. If you sign it, we'll talk. If you want me to go on the record, I want immunity." Eddy pushed away from the desk.

Cahill said, "The ASA isn't easy to get to. This may take time."

"I'm not going anywhere."

Cahill looked at me. "Let's step outside for a moment."

We left Rand's office and walked down the stairs to a deserted Canal Street. Here and there, shopkeepers were boarding up, and there were no cars on the street.

"I want to hear what he has to say," Cahill said. "Do you agree?"

"Yes. We have nothing right now. We need a break."

Before I finished my statement, he was already dialing a number on his cellphone. When someone answered the call, he said, "This is Special Agent in Charge James Cahill. I need to speak with the ASA now, if that's possible. This is regarding the Dwayne Robinson shooting in Coronado Beach." He said to me, "I'm on hold."

We both paced back and forth until someone came on the line.

"The is James Cahill with FDLE. You should have just received an email from an attorney named Eddy Rand." Cahill gave a succinct summary of the conversation we'd had with Rand. "He wants to tell us what he knows, but he wants assurances... Yes, I want to hear what he has to say. We have an explosive situation here."

Cahill paced back and forth. "Yes, I'll stay in touch." He tapped the phone screen and ended the call. "He said we could sign the agreement."

Eddy Rand was still in his office when we returned. We took our seats in front of two sheets of paper on his desk. It was the agreement Eddy wanted us to sign. We signed. He gave us copies and held the originals.

"You both know that I'm a gay man. While I'm open about it now, I spent most of my time in the closet before Ashley knew anything about it. I'd frequent a gay bar in Daytona as a way of sorting out my attraction to men. Eventually, it led to infrequent liaisons, until I met Cory Cox. I was so uncomfortable with what I was doing that I didn't give Cox my real name until we'd dated for a while. You can imagine how shocked I was that Cory worked for the Coronado Beach Police Department. Into the third month of our relationship, I was head over heels in love. I still hadn't told Ashley what was going on.

"While my affair with Cox was progressing, I began to receive compromising pictures of not only me and Cory, but pictures of the other men I'd had liaisons with before him. Finally, I received a personal letter at the firm stating that if I didn't pay the blackmailer fifty thousand dollars, they'd send the pictures to Ashley."

"And how did you manage payment?" I asked.

"I took the funds out of the law firm's general fund. Large sums go in and out of the fund continuously. So it was only a minor blip in our records. Since I oversee the fund and controlled inflows and payments, no one would know, especially not Ashley.

"I should have never paid it. I should have come clean with Ashley. But I wasn't even willing to admit to myself that I was gay, much less confess it to her. When I got the second letter demanding more money, I turned to Cory and asked for his help. We'd been together, as I said, for about three months. He wanted to know everything. I showed him the letters I'd gotten, how I'd made payment, and how I'd used the general fund to keep the payment on the QT. That was my next mistake.

"Cory managed making payment to the blackmailer through an intermediary, Dwayne Robinson.

And then, after Cory shook down Robinson, Robinson flipped on Sabatini. I was shocked when Cory told me Sabatini was the blackmailer. He did work for us, for God's sake!

"I couldn't believe it. What I knew was that I got my money back from the second extortion effort, and according to Cory, he made my problem disappear. So I was grateful. I was so grateful, I came out to Ashley and told her about my relationship with Cory.

"What I didn't know was that Cory recognized an opportunity. Through whatever means, he convinced Sabatini to join forces with him, and with the help of his muscle man Robinson, they took blackmail and extortion to the next level.

"It wasn't long after I came out that Cory asked me to do him a favor. He said he wanted to put me on retainer and pay me forty thousand dollars in advance for future legal work. I told him it wasn't necessary, I'd oversee any of his legal issues without charge. But he was insistent. So I wrote up an invoice, took his retainer and deposited the money in our firm's general fund. A month later, he said that he needed money for an emergency. But he didn't want me to give him the money; he wanted to invoice the law firm for outside security. I agreed to do it. He'd just extracted me from the clutches of Sabatini, and I was in love. I didn't see the harm. He was a cop. An exemplary cop at that. So I did it. Little did I know what a huge mistake that was.

"It wasn't a week later that he wanted to open another retainer for a client I knew was fictitious. Now we were practically living together while Ashley and I were going through our divorce. I questioned him about the transaction, which was clearly money laundering. And that's when everything turned south. He at first tried to sweet talk me into complying. When I refused, he threatened me. He knew I was in settlement talks with Ashley, and he said he'd release compromising pictures to the judge in our case, photos Sabatini had taken of me with casual sex partners from the gay bar in Daytona. I couldn't afford to have all that come out in the hearing and expose our daughter Nicole to the underside of my sexual experiments. So I caved and agreed to establish the retainer account. A week later, another invoice came from the security services company to clean up the extortion money."

Cahill asked, "So, how long did this continue?"

"When the divorce was final, Cox had nothing more to hold over my head. I broke up with him. I didn't want to be in the same room with him. But since I'd laundered money for him several times, he threatened to have me disbarred over it. I still couldn't get out from under him. What was ironic was that Cox picked the wrong man with whom to establish a business relationship. He got sideways with Sabatini, and Sabatini threatened to ruin Cox's and my careers."

"How did you know this if you and Cox weren't together anymore?" I asked.

"Sabatini came to see me at my office the day before he disappeared. He presented me with a file documenting every person they'd extorted. He had photos of Robinson engaged in collections activity and of Cox meeting Robinson to receive payments. While Sabatini was problematic, he was an excellent investigator. He built a solid case against me, Cox and Robinson. He had evidence of my involvement in laundering money for Cox. He said that Cox had failed to pay him his cut in the last several transactions. Cox had told Sabatini that he could make more money without him and no longer required his services. Sabatini flew into a rage in my office. He was furious that it was he who'd put this business together, and he was indignant that Cox would think that he could cut him out.

"He said he'd met with Cox and told him that he'd take the file to the police if he didn't pay him what he owed him. He said Cox had told him no one would take the word of a homeless investigator over the word of a decorated police officer. He'd refused to pay him.

"With that file, the police would have little difficulty charging Cox, Robinson and me with conspiracy. Three days later, Sabatini went missing."

"Why did he come to see you?"

"He threatened me with the file as well. He said if I didn't get Cox to pay him, he'd take all of us down. I told him that if he took the file to the police, he'd be implicating himself. He said that if I looked at the case he'd built closely, it showed that I had hired him to do investigations and background checks on certain people, and that Cox and Robinson were the ones engaged in extortion. The evidence would show that Sabatini had merely been doing his job as an investigator. He was convinced he could bring us all down and he'd be the hero."

Cahill said, "Seems to me Cox isn't the only one that has a motive to take Sabatini out. You also had a motive to kill him."

"That may be true, but I didn't do it!"

"How does Robinson fit into this?"

"Robinson did the collections. He'd pick money up at a drop or become an enforcer if the intended victim refused to pay. When Cox and Sabatini got sideways, Robinson was the only person, other than me, who could finger Cox and Sabatini. I can't testify to whether Cox killed Robinson or not. What I can testify to is that Cox got greedy. I can testify that Cox told me that Robinson worked for him. And I can testify that Sabatini was trying to bring Cox down, which provides a motive for his murder."

Cahlll asked, "And do you have proof that Cox and Sabatini were extorting you? Do you have proof of any of this?"

"You can follow the trail of the initial fifty thousand I paid to Sabatini. You can back up my story with circumstantial evidence, and the deposits and withdrawals from the law firm's general fund. Sabatini told me that Cox kept records of everything in a leather-bound accounting book."

"But it all comes down to your word against Cox."

"Yes, I guess it does. But I didn't shoot Dwayne Robinson. I can't say Cox murdered the two men. All I can say is he had a reason. And I wasn't anywhere near Sabatini or Robinson when someone killed them. I have alibis for both murders. Why would I make this up? This will end my law career. I just have no reason to lie."

"Other than to avoid jail time," said Cahill.

Eddy Rand didn't say anything.

I said, "If you say you weren't part of the conspiracy, why did you represent Cox? Since you knew who all the players were, and you weren't the killer, you must have known that Cox had killed Robinson to keep him quiet. If you knew he was guilty, why did you take on his defense?"

"When Cox called me from the scene of the Robinson shooting, he said that I needed to defend him or all of us would end up in jail. At that point, I didn't know that Robinson was unarmed. When you found Sabatini's body, I knew that Cox had killed him. I'd no proof, but I knew. That's when I withdrew from the case."

Cahill said, "Why didn't you come forward then?"

"Fear, mostly. Cox had already killed two men. I was the only person alive who knew the whole story. I figured I might be next. I was concerned about Nicole. I didn't know what Cox would do to ensure my silence."

"Why come forward now?" I asked.

"Cox took advantage of me at a very vulnerable time. There are things that I wish I'd done differently. I made mistakes. But they happened. I'd nothing to do with their extortion scheme, and I'd nothing to do with Sabatini's and Robinson's murders. Both Cox and Sabatini were extorting me to launder money. I'm a victim here. I only hope you'll see I was an unwilling participant in this. I want to see justice done. I'm willing to go public with what I know to see that that happens."

Cahill said, "You're willing to go public to save your ass from going to jail."

"While that may be true, I didn't have anything to do with the murders or their illegal enterprise. I made a mistake doing Cox a favor and letting him use my law firm general fund to hide money the first time. I own that. Everything after that was extortion. In exchange for my testimony, I want immunity."

Cahill said, "Write it up, and I'll take it to the state's attorney and see what he's willing to do."

"No, that's not the way this is going to work. I will not give a sworn statement or a deposition until we have a deal. Do you understand?"

"Yes. Let's work on it."

Firestorm

Rand said, "I have a sworn statement prepared that documents everything I've just told you. As soon as the ASA agrees to my immunity in writing, I'll sign the sworn statement, and if you need more, I'm prepared to give a deposition and appear in court as a witness. There's no doubt in my mind that Cox killed Sabatini and Robinson. He had motive. He had the opportunity and the means to do it. If you could find the file that Sabatini had on Cox and Robinson and the leather-bound accounting book that Cox had, along with my testimony, you've everything you need to charge and convict him."

"Do you have any idea where Cox might have kept the ledger?" Cahill asked.

"No. I didn't even know it existed until Sabatini came to see me."

"That's hearsay evidence, Mr. Rand. How valuable is that?"

"If you find it, it corroborates what I told you. Did you know about the ledger before I told you?"

"No."

"You now know to look for it. It seems to me that advances your investigation significantly. And before today, you'd no idea about the connection between Sabatini, Cox and Robinson. How valuable is that?"

After Cahill and I left Eddy Rand's office, we walked the two blocks back to the PD in silence. I called Leslie Downs and asked her to meet me in my office. She said she was in the PD and would be in my office when we arrived. I asked her to call Torres to come as well.

As I keyed in the code to enter the back entrance to the PD, Cahill said, "I need to call the ASA.

I'll be in in a minute. Jed, we need to find the Sabatini file and Cox's ledger."

26

Eddy Rand's revelations broke the case wide open. Now we could connect all the dots, but we didn't have the evidence yet to charge Cox. There was no doubt in my mind from looking at the dashcam video that Cox had intentionally shot Robinson. What we hadn't known was why. He was a decorated officer with an exemplary record. No one had wanted to believe that one of our officers would murder an unarmed man.

Now we understood why. All we had to do was prove it.

Eddy's revelations were significant for another reason. It meant that we could meet with BLM and BAP knowing the truth about what had happened. It would be much easier to assure them that we were making considerable progress in our investigation.

When I got to my office, Downs was already sitting at one of the chairs, going through a file.

She said, "I've checked Sergeant Hicks' alibi, and he was nowhere near Sabatini when he died."

"We know who killed him."

"Who?"

Before I could answer her question, Jim Cahill and Alicia Torres made their way into the office. I invited everyone to sit at the conference table.

Cahill said, "The ASA has agreed to immunize Eddy Rand. He said that he and Rand had exchanged paper and that he will have the deal done within the hour. We will have a copy of Rand's sworn statement as soon as we sign the papers."

Downs asked, "What's going on?"

Cahill pointed at me.

I went into detail on what Eddy Rand had told us and the conditions under which he'd go on the record with his testimony.

"So, we need to find the files and accounting book," Downs said.

"Sabatini didn't trust banks, made good money working for Eddy, and had that settlement from Lake Mary PD. This guy was frugal in the extreme. Where's all this money?"

Torres said, "Jed, we searched every inch of his trailer and car. We found nothing."

"Alicia, I want you to try again. Tear that trailer and Sabatini's car apart. When I say tear it apart, I want the trailer dissembled down to the bare frame. I want you to strip down the car, remove seats, take all the door panels off, and, if you have to, I want you to flip the car over and check the underside for hidden compartments. I'm willing to bet a year's pay you'll find his money in that car or trailer. And if we find his money, we will find the file with which he blackmailed Rand."

"Do you think he could have gotten a safe deposit box?" Torres asked.

"No. He was too cheap. He wouldn't have spent the money. It is in the car or trailer. I'd start with the trailer."

"Commander Morris has me scheduled for crowd control duty."

"You tell Morris that I've relieved you of that duty. I want your team to work twenty four hours if needed on this. I know you understand how important it is."

"Yep." Torres picked up her cellphone and left my office.

Downs said, "If Sergeant Hicks' police cruiser didn't make the tire tracks at Paula Cane's house..."

"Jed, didn't you tell me that Cox drove his cruiser home at night?" Cahill asked.

"We assign vehicles to detectives, sergeants and senior officers," Downs said. "They can commute from home to work if they live within the city limits. There are exceptions, but that's the policy."

I said, "When we instituted community policing, we felt having the police vehicles parked at night around the community would function as a deterrent. To answer your question directly, the department assigned Cox a vehicle."

"Where is it?" Cahill asked.

"Here, in the PD parking lot," I said with a little embarrassment that I hadn't thought about searching his car.

"If he were going to hide something in his cruiser, where would be the most obvious place?"

Downs said, "There's a deck in the trunk that you lift to access the spare. It would be easy to hide something there, or underneath the back seat."

"Now that we know Cox killed Sabatini, the tire tracks at Sabatini's trailer could have come from Cox's cruiser. He could have used the car to transport Sabatini to the murder scene. There might be forensic evidence tying Sabatini to Cox's cruiser." He said to Downs, "Get Torres to test samples of the clothing Sabatini was wearing when he was murdered against any trace evidence in the car."

Neil Jarret appeared at my door. "Banks has arranged a meeting in City Hall council chambers at one thirty with BLM and BAP organizers."

I looked at my watch. "That gives us an hour. Downs, get the key to Cox's cruiser, and let's have a look."

We walked out into the blazing August sun to the back of the parking lot. Cahill and I waited for Downs.

I asked Cahill, "What can we tell BLM and BAP about the investigation? Can we offer them anything encouraging?"

"Let's see what's in Cox's cruiser."

Downs took the long strides of a tall athlete across the parking lot, carrying keys and latex gloves for all.

We donned our gloves and walked around to the back of the car, where Downs inserted the key and opened the trunk. Nothing looked unusual. The department equipped each cruiser with safety equipment to direct traffic around an accident. Local charitable organizations provided blankets and quilts for women and children trying to leave abusive homes.

Downs and I removed everything from the trunk and placed it all on the grass behind the parking space. Careful not to disturb areas where prints might be, I lifted the thin wooden lid that covered the spare tire and pulled it out of the car. I unscrewed the wide wing nut that secured the spare to the metal floor and pulled the tire out of the car, setting it in the grass.

A Glock .22 caliber handgun and red leather-bound ledger lay where the spare had been. We decided to leave the gun and ledger in situ until crime scene techs took pictures, lifted prints and processed the gun.

Cahill said, "Torres can dust the Glock and ledger for prints and run the gun through ballistics. We can see if it matches the bullet we pulled from Sabatini."

Downs was already on the phone with Torres. "She'll be here in a minute."

I said, "Downs, would you wait here for Torres? Have her process the ledger first, then bring it to my office. Tell her as soon as she's processed the gun, I want the results immediately." I said to Cahill, "We have a meeting to get ready for."

As we walked back across the parking lot, I could hear the chants from the protesters a block and a half away. I thought about walking out in front of the PD to get a better look, but I knew the press would confront me about the case.

John Hocking had set a press conference for six p.m.

In my office, Cahill tried to dissuade me from having the meeting.

"Its scheduled. We can't pull out now—it would send the wrong message."

"Until we match the bullets from Sabatini and Cox to that gun, we can't charge Cox. It will take a couple of hours for Torres to process Cox's gun."

"What can we tell these Black leaders? I want to tell them that we've made considerable progress."

"If that gun doesn't match the bullets pulled from Sabatini and Robinson, we have nothing. We have a lot of circumstantial evidence. If the evidence doesn't support Rand's version of things, we still have a way to go before we charge Cox."

Downs came into the office with the ledger. There was black residue still clinging to the leather where they had dusted for prints. She said, "The prints on the gun, which was not issued by the department, are a match to Cox. The prints on the ledger belong to Cox, too." She said to Cahill, "Torres has gone back to the lab to oversee ballistics on the gun and to work on Sabatini's trailer and car. I did a quick scan of the ledger before I brought it in, and there are transactions between Sabatini, Robinson and Cox. I still have more research to do, but the ledger proves a connection between the three of them. If you both are okay with it, I want to spend time going through it."

Cahill said, "Until we match the bullets to the gun, all the evidence we have is that they had a business or criminal connection. We can't tie Cox to the murders, and we can't prove motive. We need to find Sabatini's file."

27

When AJ, Jarret, Cahill and I arrived at council chambers, the Black community leaders had dwindled down to Councilman Gabriel Banks and furniture dealer Eddy Brown. Two unfamiliar faces, one male and one female, were at the table. At our last meeting a couple of hours earlier, none of the Black community leaders had taken sides at the table. At this meeting, Banks, Brown and the others sat on one side of the table with their backs to the council's elevated dais. The only spaces available were on the opposite side of the table with our backs to the front of the chamber.

When I went to the end of the table to shake hands with the new folks whom I didn't know, they wouldn't extend their hands to me. When AJ, Jarret, and Cahill saw this, they took seats at the table with no effort of a greeting.

Banks started to make introductions, but the Black woman wearing a BLM T-shirt cut him off and said, "This ain't no meet and greet. I want to make that clear. I don't know what you think this meeting will accomplish. I'm Melinda Brown, and this here is Jamal Jackson."

Melinda Brown had a shaved head, a round face and large gold hoop earrings. She had a deep scar on her left cheek.

Jamal Jackson said, "If you have the notion that we're going to give you something in this meeting, you can forget it. We agreed to this meeting for one reason—to tell you what we demand. Your city council lacky," he pointed to Councilman Banks, "has spun this wonderful fantasy about how good you treat the Black man in this shitty little town. I could give a fuck. The only thing we care about is justice for Dwayne Robinson, the Black man your pig officer shot in cold blood."

Jackson had dreadlocks that hung halfway down his back. Tattoos covered his neck and arms down to his wrists. From the space that he occupied at the table, he was six-two and weighed at least two-hundred and fifty pounds.

I started to speak, but Jackson cut me off.

"I don't want to hear a word of your bullshit. Until the city council fires you and the city manager you work for, we will lay siege to this little burg, and there won't be much of it left when we leave. And I want to know why you corralled my people into that fucking park two blocks away from City Hall."

I said, "The area in front of City Hall isn't large enough to oversee a thousand people. And the press needs that area to broadcast from."

"Exactly, and that's where we're going to be. I want three hundred of our people in front of City Hall. If that doesn't happen before prime time tonight, you'll regret it. I can't control what our people might do. You get that?"

"Are you threatening us?" I asked.

He flipped his dreads over his left shoulder. "No, just telling you what'll happen."

"Our investigation is—"

Melinda Brown interrupted. "Whether you charge Officer Cox or not doesn't change anything. Dwayne Robinson is dead. And someone will pay for that. It won't be just Cox; it'll be anyone who had anything to do with it. Beginning with you, McCain. Everyone in the

171

line of authority, from the Mayor to Officer Cox, is leaving. Heads are going to roll, or the gathering of a thousand of our people could turn into an ugly mob."

Jamal Jackson said, "Here is my cellphone number." He placed a card on the table. "Call me when you open Riverside Drive in front of City Hall. If it isn't open to us at five o'clock, we'll break your barricade, and I'll lead every one of our people, all nine hundred plus, into that area."

There was silence. I weighed what I had to say carefully as I let the silence linger.

I said, "I asked for this meeting to try to avoid any potential violence. I also wanted to provide you with the assurance that we want justice for Dwayne Robinson as much as you and that we've made considerable progress in our investigation. It was my hope to convince you both that we're making every reasonable effort on Robinson's behalf. The way he died grieves me deeply.

"But let me respond to your threats. We welcome protests—peaceful protests. We set aside Riverside Park for protesters for their safety and that of the people in the community. That will not change. We will meet your threats of violence with officers who fully intend to keep the peace. We will immediately arrest anyone who engages in violence. And I assure you, Mr. Jackson, if you incite violence of any kind, we will arrest you and prosecute you to the full extent of the law. I'd hoped for a different result. But this meeting is over."

Cahill, AJ, Jarret and I stood up in unison.

As we walked out of council chambers, Jamal Jackson yelled to us, "You've made a terrible mistake."

While we walked to Jarret's office, I called Morrison and encouraged him to beef up security at

Riverside Park. He told me that he'd enough officers there to manage anything that came up. He reminded me that the department screened every person in the park for anything they could use as a weapon.

We took seats around Jarret's table.

Cahill said, "While I applaud you standing up to Jackson and Brown, the thing I feared has happened. We've made this personal. We've poked the bear, and I feel like we made it worse."

"I don't agree, Jim, Jarret said. "If we hadn't met, we would've had no idea they might attempt to break out of Riverside Park. Jed stood up to them and said they aren't going to push us around."

Cahill said, "The whole strategy behind FDLE conducting the investigation into the Robinson shooting was to insulate you from all the drama. Now, Jed, you've become the target of their anger."

"I was the target of their anger because I'm the chief," I said. "Cox worked for me. There's no way you can insulate me from that, Jim."

"What're you going to do to keep this from becoming violent?" AJ asked.

"We need to move quickly. The only thing that will take the wind out of BLM and Jamal Jackson is to charge Cox with murder. Once that happens, the press will lose interest until a trial. If we can announce his arrest at the six p.m. presser, that will steal the press coverage away from Jackson."

Cahill said, "That doesn't give us much time."

"Jim, you and I can work Sabatini's files with Torres. By the time we get to the lab, Torres should have ballistics on the gun completed. Downs is working on Cox's ledger." I said to everyone, "It's three o'clock. Let's reconvene at five."

I thanked AJ for being at the meeting.

Cahill and I left Jarret's office and walked across the parking lot to the PD. We went to my office. Cahill immediately jumped on his cellphone and sat in my desk chair, and I left to find Downs. She was on the second floor in the detective's bull pen, reading Cox's ledger.

She asked, "Any luck with the protest leaders?"

"No. What're you finding in the ledger?"

"I was wrong. There was nothing tying Sabatini to Cox's ledger. In fact, there are no entries that specifically mention Sabatini. It does document all the funds received from Robinson, and the funds ran through the Rand Law Firm. It proves that money was flowing from Robinson and that Rand laundered the money through his law firm's general fund. It shows the retainer accounts and the invoices Cox submitted to the law firm for bogus security services. We have Cox and Rand for fraud and money laundering. Extortion will be difficult to prove with these records, since Cox didn't list the people he extorted. With what we have, we can send Cox to prison, but we don't have enough to charge him with two murders."

"I want you to call the ASA and explain that we're close to bringing charges against Cox and we need him to attend the meeting at five. On the ledger, keep digging. Be prepared to put evidence together for the ASA."

I left the detectives' bull pen, walked downstairs and met Cahill standing in the doorway of my office, waiting for me. We walked out into the parking lot, jumped into my unmarked cruiser and drove the two blocks to Torres' crime lab. In the back of the building was a large open garage facility. In the middle of the floor sat the bare frame of the old Shasta travel trailer. Torres' crew had totally disassembled it.

I asked one of the techs where Torres was. He called her on his cellphone, and in less than a minute, she walked out of the building and into the garage.

Before I could ask her how it was going, Torres said, "I found it. I found Sabatini's folder and his money. You could take me out for a drink tonight, and then later you could show me appreciation."

Ignoring her flirting, I said, "Where was it?"

She sashayed over to the trailer frame and pointed to a steel box someone had welded on top of it.

Torres said, "Underneath each of the bench seats in the small dinette is a storage compartment. One of them had a false plywood bottom. When I removed it, it opened into the steel box welded to the underside of the frame. If we hadn't taken the trailer apart, we'd have never found it."

"What was in there?"

"There was a shade over half a million dollars in that compartment. I've never seen that amount of money in one place before. It was all in hundred dollar bills. And with it, we found the folder you were looking for. I just scanned through it, but it documents all the people they were blackmailing, including the file Sabatini was keeping on Cox, Robinson and Rand. I need to spend more time with it, but it looks like the smoking gun.

"A couple more things. Now that we know the connection between Robinson, Cox and Sabatini, there are prepaid cellphone calls between Robinson, Cox and Sabatini's burner phones. Sabatini was digging up dirt on people and giving it to Cox, who would initiate the blackmail, and Robinson was doing their collections. Sabatini had the whole scheme documented with pictures, field notes and his own copies of the material they were using to extort people. He also had information tying Eddy Rand into the scheme."

"Good work, Torres. Be at my office at five to present this information to the ASA."

"I'm not done yet. We found epithelia on the black plastic bags Sabatini's body was wrapped in. The DNA is a match for Cory Cox. We also found hair in Sabatini's trailer that's a match for Cox. So, we can prove that Cox broke into the trailer looking for Sabatini's file. We also found fibers in the back seat of Cox's cruiser that are a match to the shirt Sabatini was wearing when Cox buried him. And the file provides the motive. Sabatini was trying to blackmail Cox, and that got him killed. Cox killed Robinson to shut him up. He knew too much."

"Ballistics?" I asked.

"The striations on the bullets found in Sabatini match the gun we found in Cox's police cruiser."

"Great job."

"So, what about that drink?" She pulled off her crime scene ballcap and let her hair fall past her shoulders.

"Torres, you need to quit that," Cahill said.

Torres nodded at me and said, "He loves it."

I smiled, and Cahill shook his head. "McCain, we have work to do." He said to Torres, "Nice work."

As we left the crime lab, I was thinking that creating our own crime lab was one of the best decisions I had ever made. Despite her flirtatious persona, Torres was a brilliant officer. Shortly after we'd hired her and her team, she'd purchased equipment that could turn DNA testing around in two hours. The fact that Torres could focus her crew on this investigation without distraction was an enormous benefit. If we had had to wait for support from the FDLE crime lab in Orlando, it would have been days or weeks before results would be available.

I said to Cahill, "We have enough to charge Cox with murder. Downs said the ASA is in possession of Rand's signed sworn statement. He emailed us both a copy. We should show it to Cox when we interview him."

The overwhelming caseload at the ASA's office in Daytona made it difficult to get warrants in a timely manner. Asking to have an ASA in my office was without precedent. But given the nature of the case and the potential impact on the community, and the need to advance the case in the face of violent protests, I hoped the ASA would answer Downs' call for help.

28

When we got to my office, it was approaching the five o'clock hour when Jamal Jackson had threatened violence if we didn't let his protesters move from Riverside Park to the front of City Hall and the PD. I'd already called Morris to get an update on his efforts to reinforce police numbers at the park. He assured me he could handle anything that came his way.

I said, "I'm concerned, since the park backs up to the Indian River, that the docks in the park could be used by boats to supply the protesters with weapons."

"Jed, we anticipated all of that. We have police and sheriff's boats keeping boats away from the park, and we have people at the docks to prevent that from happening."

"Any sign of an attempt to break out of the park?"

"Melinda Brown and Jamal Jackson are whipping up the crowd with a message of hate toward the police. The crowd is showing their disdain for the police with insults and banners condemning police brutality. It is a raucous scene, but peaceful for now. Beyond that, everything is under control."

I picked up the card Jamal Jackson had given me. I thought about calling him with the hope of heading off a problem. I thought about telling him we were about to charge Cox with murder and to be patient. But I knew that they weren't here for justice for Dwayne Robinson. They were here to advance their own agenda. Gabriel

Banks had had it right from the beginning. They were here for the scalps they hoped to take as a measure of their power. This was much bigger than Dwayne Robinson and this "shitty little town."

As I was setting Jackson's card down on the desk, Jim Cahill walked into my office, along with Alicia Torres.

I said, "I could use a little good news, Jim."

"I have excellent news," Cahill said. "I want to wait until everyone is here, and I'll go through it. But not only do we have enough to bring charges against Cox, we have enough evidence to convict beyond a reasonable doubt."

"Are you overseeing the press conference at six?"

"I think you should delay it for an hour or so. It would be nice to interview Cox with the information we have before we meet with the press. I asked one of my agents to bring Cox in for questioning."

"We should talk about it," I said. "If we can announce at shortly after six that we've arrested Cox for the murders, it would hit the local news and the national news at six-thirty p.m. and would go a long way to defuse the crowd down the street. If we wait until seven p.m., it will be eleven before the news will break."

"Are we interrupting anything?" Downs asked, standing at the doorway with ASA Wesley Oglethorpe in tow.

"Come in, come in." I extended my hand to Oglethorpe. "Wes, it's good to see you."

Oglethorpe said, "I hope you all have enough to make this outing worthwhile."

We all pulled out chairs around the conference table and sat down.

Firestorm

Downs, Cahill and Torres went through the evidence they had collected thus far. It took half an hour to review everything, shuffling paper back and forth to the ASA.

Oglethorpe was five-seven and overweight, had a full head of neatly trimmed medium-brown hair and wore a full beard to hide a double chin. He wore a dark blue suit with a red tie and a pocket square. His light brown eyes peered out over cheater glasses perched on the end of his nose.

Oglethorpe said, "Looks like an excellent case. I've no doubt you have the evidence to support first degree murder charges for both Sabatini and Robinson with special circumstances."

"Not to exclude money laundering, bank fraud, extortion and other charges," Cahill added.

I said, "I've got angry protesters, a rabid press, and a press conference looming in twenty minutes. I'd like Cahill to tell them that we've charged Cox and be able to disclose the outline of our case, without going into details."

"Where's Cox now?" Oglethorpe asked.

Cahill said, "I just got a text from my agent that he's in the PD interview room. And he has a new attorney. With Eddy Rand deeply involved, he recused himself from the case."

"I'm signing this arrest warrant for first degree murder. Once you take Cox into custody, Agent Cahill, you can announce his arrest at the press conference. You can say that we arrested him for the murders of Sabatini and Robinson, but you can't go into detail until we put all the paperwork together." Oglethorpe pulled his reading glasses off. "Cox has the right to hear why we're charging him."

Cahill said, "We won't have time to do that before the presser."

"After the press conference, while I'm here, we should go over our case with him and get his statement. We should try to get a confession. The evidence is overwhelming."

"Why would he confess?" Downs asked.

Oglethorpe said, "The cold-blooded way Cox shot Sabatini and Robinson makes Cox eligible for the death penalty. He may be willing to plea for life without parole in exchange for a confession. Given the circus that surrounds this case and the potential for a protracted trial, I've no problem taking the death penalty off the table in exchange for a guilty plea and full confession. As explosive as the situation is, I'm putting a short fuse on this offer.

"Given the weight of the case, I'll lead the interview. Jim, you'll present the evidence. After we give Cox the opportunity to respond to the charges, I'll explain the deal we're prepared to offer him." Oglethorpe turned toward me. "I assume you want to participate?"

"Yes. And Commander Downs collected much of the evidence. I'd like her in there as well."

"All right. I need time to put the charging paperwork together and to grab a bite. Can we reconvene at seven?"

We all agreed.

Oglethorpe said, "Arrest Cox, book him, and have him back in the interview room by seven. Where can I set up? I have work to do."

I said, "Use my office. If you need anything, I'll ask Martha to stay for an hour or two."

"I won't need her. You need to get moving."

Firestorm

Downs, Cahill and I went to the interview room. Cox and a man I didn't know occupied one side of the table. The three of us filed in. The attorney with Cox introduced himself as James Scott.

Scott stood, took off his black horn-rimmed glasses and said, "You picked my client up at his home and brought him here without explanation. Why is he here?"

Cahill said, "Cory Cox, we're arresting you for the murders of Sabastian Sabatini and Dwayne Robinson." Cahill read Cox his Miranda rights.

"On what grounds do you bring these charges?" Scott asked.

"We're going to book Sergeant Cox and return him to this interview room. At seven, we will meet with you and your client and present our evidence. Also present at the meeting at seven will be ASA Oglethorpe."

I said to Downs, "Would you book Sergeant Cox?"

TV camera crews, photographers and reporters filled the PD parking lot. News crews jammed the lectern with microphones and voice recorders. After charging Cox, we started the presser seven minutes late.

Ron Hocking introduced Cahill, and Cahill stepped up to the podium. Chants and shouts from the protesters a block away filled the air. Reporters jockeyed for position around the lectern, raising their voices in conversation. As soon as Cahill began to speak, there was immediate silence as reporters strained to hear over the protesters in the park.

"As of five forty-five this evening, we arrested Sergeant Cory Cox and charged him with the first-degree murders of Sabastian Sabatini and Dwayne Robinson. Cox, Sabatini and Robinson were engaged in a conspiracy to extort money from members of the community. When their business relationship went sideways, Cox murdered his two partners to keep his involvement from becoming public. In addition to murder charges, we anticipate bringing additional charges related to their criminal activities.

"Our investigation is moving forward with unprecedented speed, and we aren't at liberty to disclose any details at this time. We've no doubt that Cox committed these murders, and we will prosecute him to the full extent of the law. Cory Cox is in custody, and we are processing him now.

"I'd be happy to take some questions."

Cahill pointed to Charles Knight.

"Agent Cahill, BLM and Blacks Against Police Brutality are demanding the resignation of Chief McCain and Neil Jarret, the city manager. They say they can't control what their protesters might do if you don't meet his demands. How do you respond to that?"

"Let me begin by saying there's no evidence that Cox shot Robinson for racial reasons. This was not a racially inspired murder. Cox shot Robinson to keep him quiet. They were both involved in a criminal conspiracy. Cox's motive had everything to do with greed and avoiding arrest. Cox was a bad cop. Robinson was a thug Cox used to do his dirty work. The murder had nothing to do with Cox being a cop or the fact that Robinson was Black. As far as the threat of violence is concerned, I can't control what the protesters might do. As you can see, there's a considerable police presence in the city. They're here to keep the peace. We respect the right of anyone to protest peacefully. If they choose violence, we will not hesitate to arrest and prosecute them."

Knight followed up with, "All of this happened under McCain and Jarret's watch. Don't you think they bear responsibility?"

"No. There hasn't been a scrap of evidence of a failure of either leadership or policy. The simple fact is Cory Cox chose a criminal path. He broke trust. The blame, if we need to blame someone, falls directly on the shoulders of Cory Cox. That's who we arrested and charged. Dwayne Robinson and Sabastian Sabatini also share the blame. They all willingly participated in an illegal conspiracy with Cox. No one forced them to do it."

Cahill pointed to another reporter.

"Angela Bishop, *Wall Street Journal*. One of McCain's people shot Robinson in cold blood. Doesn't that mean anything?"

Cahill said, "What happened to Dwayne Robinson was tragic. Cox shot the man in cold blood. He and he alone is to blame for what he did. As law enforcement officers, we place blame by charging those who commit crimes and prosecute them. In this case, with the evidence we have, I assure you that we will prosecute Cory Cox. Tomorrow we will have more details about the case. But for now, we're bringing a criminal to justice for the barbaric murders he committed."

Bishop followed up with, "A murder trial could last for months. Are you concerned that the protests could continue until there's a verdict? Just because you charge him with murder doesn't mean you will obtain a conviction."

"While I can't go into the details of the case, I can say with confidence that we have evidence that proves beyond any reasonable doubt that Cox murdered Robinson and Sabatini. The evidence is irrefutable. Again, I can't predict what the protesters might do. Our officers will remain in sufficient force to protect the city from violence. Those who wish to protest peacefully are welcome to do so. That's their right."

A reporter yelled, "Jamie Daniels, Fox News."

Cahill acknowledged Daniels.

"We've learned that the department nearly fired Chief McCain twice since taking over as chief three years ago. I remember covering a serial killer who followed McCain to Florida and resumed his killing spree here in Coronado Beach. And my sources tell me that the city manager almost fired McCain for breach of protocol as chief last year. Now we have this spectacular case drawing national attention to Coronado Beach once again."

Cahill tried to break in, but Daniels yelled over him.

"There's sentiment on the city council to sever ties with McCain. They're concerned about the threats of violence. How would you respond?"

"Let me begin with the serial killings three years ago. While the killer had a previous connection with McCain while he was a detective for the New York Police Department, there's no way that McCain could control the behavior of a madman. It was through his excellent police work that he found the killer. FDLE lost one of its finest senior officers bringing the killer to justice.

Firestorm

"A year ago, again through no fault of Chief McCain, he uncovered a flaw in intradepartmental reporting procedures. He fixed the procedure. While we aired disagreements about the procedure, there was never any serious discussion of McCain's dismissal as chief.

"Today, through no fault of the chief, a rogue, corrupt police officer committed murder. There isn't a chief of police on the planet who could have prevented that from happening."

Daniels yelled over the crowd again, "If McCain had tighter control over his officers, this might not have happened."

Cahill said, "I don't mean to be disrespectful, but that might be true in an ideal fantasy world. Coronado Beach Police Department is too small to afford internal affairs investigators. But even the departments that do can't prevent corruption. Internal affairs exists to pursue corrupt cops after the fact. Cox had a clean record. He was a decorated officer. Why he chose to engage in criminal activities, we don't know. But we've dealt with Cox swiftly. This investigation has moved without prejudice or favor. Chief McCain is a fine officer. He had an exemplary record with the NYPD as a homicide detective. There's no hint of any racial issues with this case or Chief McCain's management of the department. The City of Coronado Beach is lucky to have Chief McCain. This is the last question I'll answer along this line."

Cahill took questions for another ten minutes. The questions related to evidence he was unable to reveal. He kept reassuring the press that Cox had murdered Robinson and that the murder had nothing to do with race.

"Thank you," he finally said to the press, and he turned around and stepped away from the lectern, ignoring the reporters' shouted questions.

As Cahill approached me, I said, "You managed that beautifully."

"It doesn't matter what you think," he replied. "It's what they write."

I got a call from a number I recognized: Jamal Jackson. I told Cahill I'd meet him in my office, and I answered the call.

Firestorm

29

Jamal Jackson said, "I'm assuming you called me to tell me that you and the city manager are resigning and that my people can protest in front of City Hall."

I ignored his statement. "I called to give you a heads up that we've charged Cory Cox with the first-degree murder of Dwayne Robinson and one other man. You said earlier that you wanted justice for Robinson. Cox, Robinson and another man participated in an extortion scheme. Things got sideways, and Cox killed Robinson to shut him up. Cox was a dirty cop. If your presence in Coronado Beach is about justice for Robinson, then this news should please you."

"You must have been born in a hayfield. Do you honestly believe I care about what happened to Robinson? Or what happens to Cox? Your cop shot an unarmed Black man. That's the headline. And the only thing that matters here is headlines. A White man shot a Black man, and someone is going to pay."

I said, "Cox will pay. With the evidence we have, he'll spend the rest of his life in prison."

"That isn't a headline we can recruit or raise money with. We need trophies to hold up to the country. We need trophies to show the Black man that we speak for them. One of those trophies can be the riots and looting that will take place later tonight. That makes headlines. Those trophies could be you and the city manager resigning. I really don't give a fuck which one. But one way or the other, we're going to get our headline. How we do that is up to you. When we get off the phone, Councilman Banks will hear from me. I'm going to tell him that I'm not leaving town without a trophy. I'm certain when the city council understands the choice, they'll have one less city manager and police chief."

I said, "This has nothing to do with justice. This has to do with power."

"You're finally catching on. The White man has lorded over the Black man for more than two hundred years. Where was justice then? Where was the justice in slavery? Where's the justice in that one-fifth of the Black population lives in poverty? That's double that of the White man. Don't talk to me about justice. This is about power. You have until eight tonight."

The phone went dead.

It was seven. I walked into my office, and ASA Oglethorpe, Leslie Downs and Cahill were looking through case files.

Cahill said, "Cox and his attorney are waiting in the interview room. All the equipment is set up. We were waiting for you."

I said, "Wes and Leslie, could you give the room to Jim and me for a minute, please?"

"Sure," she said.

Oglethorpe gathered his files, and Downs escorted him out of my office.

"What's up, Jed?" Cahill asked.

"Jamal Jackson called me. I told him that we charged Cox with first-degree murder. His demands haven't changed. He wants Jarret and me fired, or he's threatening to burn the town to the ground. He said he was calling Banks and giving the city council to eight p.m. to fire Jarret and me or the crowd would become violent."

"Did he say anything more about moving the protest to City Hall?"

"No."

Cahill said, "He's backing down, Jed. And we've more than enough officers to prevent violence."

"You and I know that, but the council doesn't."

"What makes you so sure that the council will take this seriously?"

"The council consists of shopkeepers, a teacher, a pastor, a retired businessman and others who have no idea what Jamal Jackson is capable of," I said. "They're laypeople who'll be easily frightened."

"Do you want to put Cox off until morning to deal with this?"

"No. But I do want to call AJ and give him a heads up."

"Call him, and let's get this interview with Cox done."

Just as I was about to call AJ, I got a call from him.

"Banks is calling for an emergency city council meeting tonight at eight," he told me.

"Let me guess—Jamal Jackson."

"Yes, and you and Jarret are topic A. I want you there to defend yourself."

"I don't want to do that. I don't want to have to convince anyone to keep my job. I want to be here because they want me here. I'm not going to lobby anyone. If they fire me, and that brings peace, so be it."

"What about Jarret? Who'll defend him?"

"You will. He reports directly to you and the council. Given the controversy surrounding me, my endorsement of Neil might drive a nail into his coffin. You defend him."

"Jackson wants us to fire you both," AJ said.

"Don't worry about me. I have a nice pension. Worry about Jarret. He has a family to feed."

"I don't want to remain mayor if you're not chief anymore. The only reason I've hung around is to help you and Neil."

"Thanks, AJ. You've been a great friend. I owe you so much. But I want you to know that regardless of what happens, I'll be fine. If my leaving gives comfort to the council, don't fight it. If you can save Neil's job, tell Jackson he can have me but not Neil. AJ, I need to go. We have Cox waiting in an interview room, and I need to question him."

AJ said, "I hope you're doing the right thing."

"Whatever happens to me is okay, AJ. Focus on Jarret."

"Before you go, I've one question for you. Do you feel you have sufficient police resources to prevent the crowd from turning violent?"

"Yes, I do. But if you're asking me to guarantee there won't be violence..."

"I understand. Thanks, Jed."

30

Sergeant Martha Johnson had prepared the largest of the three interview rooms with a table and six chairs, a video camera, microphones, sound recording equipment, a pitcher of ice water and six glasses.

Leslie Downs, Jim Cahill, Oglethorpe and I filed past an officer standing guard and entered the room. Cory Cox sat next to his attorney, James Scott. Oglethorpe and Scott addressed each other by their first names. We all sat at the table.

The windowless interview room had no pictures on the walls or anything that might distract during an interrogation.

Since we'd taken Cox's initial statement the night of the Robinson shooting, Cahill had thought it was a waste of time to bring Cox back in for questioning until we had evidence that either convicted or cleared him.

At over six feet, Cox towered over his attorney, who had a slight build and closely cut blond hair. He barely looked old enough to have graduated from law school. Cox and Scott sat across from us.

ASA Oglethorpe began. "Downs, would you turn on the recording equipment?"

Oglethorpe gave a verbal inventory of those in attendance, the time, the case number and the charges against Cox. "Has Mr. Cox been read his Miranda rights?"

Downs said, "He has."

"Mr. Cox, we have charged you with the first-degree murders of Sabastian Sabatini and Dwayne Robinson. To be more specific, you executed them with premeditation that under Florida law qualifies for special circumstances. As a police officer, you're held to a higher standard. For those reasons, we will seek the death penalty in your case. Do you wish to say anything?"

Scott said, "I've advised my client not to answer your questions. We will answer all questions with 'no comment.'"

"Very well," Oglethorpe said. "Sergeant Cox, you've the right to remain silent. But Coronado Beach is under siege by those who wish to harm this community because of the heinous crimes you committed. Because of the explosive circumstances we find ourselves in, I'm here to underscore how important this moment is for you. Special Agent Cahill is going to lay out our case to you and counselor Scott. At the conclusion, we will give you the opportunity to acknowledge your guilt and give us a full confession. In exchange, we're prepared to take the death penalty off the table and offer you a life sentence without parole. This plea agreement, which I have with me, is ready for you and your attorney to sign."

John Scott said, "You can't expect my client to accept a plea under such duress. The confession would never stand up in court."

"Counselor, before you raise objections, wait until Cahill presents the case they have." Oglethorpe nodded to Cahill to begin.

Cahill said, "You, Sabatini and Robinson were engaged in a conspiracy to extort money from prominent members of the community. Sabatini investigated these victims and dug up dirt on them, then you extorted them using email. Robinson did the collection work. Then you got greedy. You thought you could cut Sabatini out and do the investigative work yourself. Sabatini had created the model. After you understood the pattern, you and Robinson branched out on your own. Adding insult to injury, you withheld payment from Sabatini on the last three extortion victims. My guess is you thought you could get away with it since Sabatini couldn't go to the police without implicating himself.

"You messed with the wrong guy. You hadn't counted on Sabatini documenting everything that you did, including photographing and videotaping your and Robinson's activities. You didn't count on him building an airtight case against you, Robinson and Eddy Rand. When Sabatini threatened to blackmail you with his files, you realized the damage he could do to you. You could have just paid him what you owed him, but you realized how unstable Sabatini was. You understood that even if you paid him, that would never be the end of it.

"Between your ledger, Sabatini's files and Eddy Rand's general funds records, we estimate that you extorted over one million dollars from ten victims. With what you withheld from Sabatini, your share, including what you paid Robinson for collection work, totals nearly six hundred thousand. With Sabatini out of the way, the money was all yours. You concluded that Sabatini had to go. The files he had on you, Robinson and Rand were too damaging to let him live.

"Four days ago, you went to Sabatini's camping trailer in your police cruiser and cuffed him at gunpoint. You broke into his trailer and searched for the files he had on you. When you didn't find them, you drove Sabatini to a fire road on the edge of town, shot him and buried him in a shallow grave. We know that you drove the city cruiser because tire tread marks at the scene match your vehicle. We found strands of your hair in Sabatini's camper that are a match to your DNA. Clothing fibers found in the rear seat of your assigned cruiser matched clothing Sabatini was wearing when you shot him. Epithelial cells and sweat droplets found on the garbage bags you used to wrap up Sabatini's body match your DNA and tie you to the crime scene.

"After we searched his trailer the second time, we found a metal box welded to the underside of the trailer. Under the seats in the dinette, there was a storage compartment with a fake plywood bottom that, when removed, provided access to the metal box under the floor. Inside, we found a hefty sum of cash and the files Sabatini used to confront you and Eddy Rand. These files document your extortion operation in fine detail, with pictures and video of your meetings with Robinson.

"Inside your assigned cruiser, we found two crucial pieces of evidence hidden under the spare tire. First, we found a .22 caliber handgun we can prove fired the bullet found in Sabatini's head. We also found this ledger," Cahill held up a red leather-bound accounting book, "which shows payments made to Robinson under the guise of security services. It also shows revenues you deposited in Rand's general fund recorded as retainer fees. These match those transactions recorded in Eddy Rand's law firm's general fund. The ledger also shows payments made to Sabatini.

Firestorm

"Inside your home, we found a laptop computer. Even though you erased the hard drive, we were able to retrieve emails you sent to your victims, demanding money. Attached to the emails were pictures showing the victims engaged in compromising activities and the details of your extortion.

"In addition, we've sworn testimony from Eddy Rand that corroborates the evidence, and he offered detailed testimony about his involvement in the conspiracy and how you blackmailed him into participation.

"We have the dashcam video of you shooting Robinson. We can clearly see you moving between the dashcam and Robinson. In fact, it is obvious from the video that you shuffled sideways, blocking the view of the camera before you shot him. Given the rest of the evidence, it is clear you were mopping up your operation and that Robinson, like Sabatini, became a liability."

While Cahill was going through the evidence, he passed copies of the documentation to Cox and Scott. Downs played the dashcam video several times, while Cahill pointed out the obvious move Cox had made to obstruct the view of the dashcam.

Cahill paused and pushed his chair away from the interview table. "So, what do you have to say for yourself?"

Cox began to speak, and Scott cut him off.

"I want a copy of the charging documents. As I said a moment ago, you will not push my client into a plea deal just because you have an angry mob at your door. That isn't my client's problem."

Oglethorpe said, "Sergeant Cox, you've one chance and one chance only for a reduced sentence. I'll give you a half-hour to consult with your attorney. Given the evidence we have, you'd be a fool not to take the deal."

Oglethorpe announced the conclusion of the interview and nodded to Downs to turn off all the equipment. Turning to Cox's attorney, he said, "Counselor, you have thirty minutes."

In my office, Downs excused herself to see if Tom Morris could use her help. Oglethorpe, Cahill and I gathered around my desk. I reached into the desk drawer, extracted a half bottle of Makers' Mark whiskey and three glasses, and poured two fingers into the tumblers.

All three of us tossed back the drink in one effort and set the glasses on the desk. No one wanted a refill, so I put the bottle back in the desk drawer.

Martha Johnson appeared at my door. "AJ McFarland called. He wants you and Agent Cahill in council chambers right now. He said he's holding up the meeting until you're both there."

Oglethorpe said, "This have anything to do with BLM wanting you fired?"

"How did you know, Wes?" I asked.

"Jed, it's all over the news. I don't care what outlet you turn to, you see Jamal Jackson demanding that the city council clean house—you and Jarret. It sounds like they're meeting now."

"Tell the mayor we're on the way."

"I can manage Cox," Oglethorpe said. "You need to take care of business."

31

When Jim Cahill and I arrived at the council chambers, members of the council were sitting at their seats behind the dais. AJ was pacing back and forth behind his tall chair in the center. Councilman Banks and Eddy Brown were conversing in the back of the room. Melinda Brown from BLM and Jamal Jackson with BAP were in a corner of the room in conference. The Black leaders we had met with previously sat in chairs reserved for the public. And there was a handful of people seated in chambers. I also noticed that there was no press or cameras at the meeting.

Under the Florida Sunshine Law, public meetings were required to be open to the public, and the council had to give the public reasonable notice. Given the dire situation of the threat of violence, we had no time to give the public notice and would debate the question later.

AJ took his chair and gaveled the meeting to order. Everyone took their seats. Cahill and I sat at the back of the room.

AJ said, "This emergency meeting of the City Council of Coronado Beach has been called to address the demands of Black Lives Matter and Blacks Against Police Brutality—"

Before AJ could finish his sentence and state the purpose of the meeting, Jamal Jackson stood, pointed to AJ and yelled, "We're going to cut the bullshit. You either fire Jed McCain right now, or I can't be responsible for what'll happen to your little town. One of your White officers shot an unarmed Black man in cold blood. I don't give a fuck what the reason was. Dwayne Robinson is dead. Chief McCain is going to pay the price."

"Are you threatening us?" AJ asked.

"No, I'm not threatening you. I'm stating a fucking fact. If you don't fire McCain, you'll have riots and looting tonight, and every person on this council is to blame, not me."

Councilman Banks said, "If it were up to me, I'd have you arrested now for threatening police officers and city officials. And if you don't sit down and let this council conduct its business, I'll call for a vote to arrest you, and I have the votes to do it. Now sit down, and you will not interrupt this meeting again." Then Banks addressed Melinda Brown. "Ms. Brown, do you also wish to threaten this council?"

"No, Councilman. But your White officer unnecessarily took the life of a Black man. As a Black man, if anyone should understand the injustice in that, you should. This is so typical of the violence suffered by Black people in our country today at the hands of White police. Like it or not, Chief McCain is responsible for what happened. You can't stand by and do nothing. Justice demands that someone pay for what happened. Our protests so far have been peaceful because our people believe that you will do the right thing. If someone's head doesn't roll at this meeting, I've no idea what'll happen. That isn't a threat, just my understanding of the reality of the situation. People are angry. You need to consider that in your deliberations.

"Mr. Jackson and I have said what we came to say. What happens to the protesters that fill your city park tonight is in your hands." Melinda Brown stood. "Jamal, we're finished here."

Jamal Jackson stood and followed Melinda Brown out of the council chambers and out of the building.

AJ said, "As I was trying to say, this meeting concerns the demands of BLM and BAP that you just heard, that we fire Chief McCain. We called this emergency meeting without providing the public adequate notice, so the council can take no official action. Which means that even if we wanted to fire Chief McCain, we can't do it at this meeting. What we can do is communicate to Chief McCain whether we have continued confidence in him to continue to serve as chief. We will do this through an informal vote of confidence. A vote of no confidence would indicate our desire to have the chief resign. If he chooses not to resign, then as soon as we can schedule a properly called meeting, the council can take official action. Knowing Chief McCain, in the face of a no confidence vote, he'd voluntarily resign.

"I'd like to open it to discussion before we take a vote. Chief McCain, can you give us an update on the investigation?"

I said, "Since FDLE has led this investigation, the proper protocol would be for Jim Cahill to address that question." I turned to Cahill. "You're up."

Cahill stood and walked forward. "We charged Cory Cox this evening with two counts of murder in the first degree with special circumstance. This means that we can seek the death penalty for these two executions. Cox, Sabatini and Robinson were engaged in a criminal conspiracy to extort money from wealthy members of our community. Their business relationship fell apart, and Cox, trying to avoid arrest, murdered Sabatini and Robinson to keep them quiet. That's the condensed version. The case is more complicated than that. We not only have physical evidence that proves the case against Cox beyond any reasonable doubt, but we also have direct witness testimony to back up our case.

"Due to the present hostile environment, we've offered Cox a plea bargain, life in prison without parole in exchange for a confession. If we take the case to court, we will seek the death penalty. Given the convincing evidence, it is my belief that the court will easily convict him. We gave Cox thirty minutes to accept or reject the offer."

Gabriel Banks asked, "In your view, was this preventable? Is there any action the department could have taken to catch this before it led to people losing their lives? You know the Robinsons will sue the city for wrongful death. Were we negligent in any way?"

"We still have to complete our investigation, but so far, we haven't found a sliver of evidence that the department acted with negligence."

AJ said, "Then who's to blame? Is the chief to blame?"

"I think that's a question for the chief to answer," Cahill said. "It is his job on the line, and I think he should have an opportunity to speak before you take a vote. In my view, you couldn't find a better chief of police than Jed McCain. He's not to blame here."

Eddy Brown stood up and said, "Before Chief McCain talks, I'd like to offer a perspective as a member of the Black community. Since McCain became chief, the relationship between our community and the police department has improved dramatically. What happened to Dwayne Robinson had nothing to do with race. All of those men made the choice to engage in illegal activity.

"Cory Cox is a corrupt officer. He made the decision to violate the law. He and he alone is to blame for the murder of Robinson.

"Robinson was a hardened criminal. He chose this path. He made the choice to engage in extortion with Cox. He put himself in harm's way. He's to blame." Eddy Brown sat down.

Banks said, "We don't have a blame problem. Cox murdered Robinson in cold blood. He's to blame. We have a political problem. To the Jamal Jacksons and Melinda Browns, while they may raise the issue of blame, what they care about is the politics. Dwayne Robinson means nothing to them. The progress this city has made to improve race relations means nothing to them. The efforts of this police chief to change discriminatory policies and procedures that have reduced crime and arrests of our Black young men means nothing to these organizations. This is political. The easy way out is to sacrifice a fine young man and make him the scapegoat to appease the political demands of these radical organizations. That would be easy. We send Chief McCain on his way, and the protesters leave with a trophy. The problem is that it isn't right. I don't think there's a person on this council who believe that Jed McCain is responsible for what happened with Cox or Robinson."

The room fell silent. AJ waited an appropriate amount of time to give someone else the opportunity to speak. When no one said anything, he said, "Chief McCain, do you have something to say before the council votes?"

I stood up, moved into the aisle and approached the dais. "Thanks to you, Councilman Banks and Mr. Brown, for your supportive comments. Given the situation, they mean a great deal to me.

"I agree with Councilman Banks—we're dealing with a political issue. I also agree that whether Cox confesses or not has no value to BLM and BAP. As Councilman Banks told me yesterday, they are looking for a scalp, a trophy. The potential for violence is real, though. While we've done everything possible to secure our city, I can't guarantee that it won't erupt into something we can't control.

"While I don't feel I could control Cox's corruption, I'm the chief, and the buck stops with me. He worked for me, and he murdered a man on my watch. I can't change that.

"Certainly, the needs of the community outweigh my need for continued employment. If my removal as chief will ensure that no violence will come to the city, I'd totally support you removing me as chief. And if you ask me to resign, I will without hesitation. Your responsibility is to protect the citizens of this city, and that's your highest priority."

I hesitated to say more. I sat back down beside Cahill.

AJ said, "Chief McCain, if you wouldn't mind leaving chambers while we consider this, I'd appreciate it."

I stood, Cahill stood with me, and we left. I felt at peace. Whether I stayed or not, I'd done all I could do.

When Cahill and I got back to my office, Oglethorpe was packing to leave. "Cox has taken the deal. Part of the agreement is that he provides a complete and thorough statement of what happened. We will also require him to elocute to the judge prior to sentencing. We reduced the plea deal to paper, and Cox, his attorney, a witness and I signed it. You can finish in the morning."

Cahill asked, "Can we disclose his confession to the press?"

"Yes. Given the state of things in town, the sooner the better. Gents, I need to run."

I sent a text to AJ, telling him that Cox had confessed. I got no response.

Cahill said, "If there's nothing more tonight, I'm headed home. I'll see you in the morning.

They left me alone in my office. I called Tom Morris. He said that things were under control at Riverside Park and that there were no signs that violence was about to erupt.

I said, "If there's going to be a problem, it will be tonight. Don't let your guard down." I told him that I wanted to have a meeting with staff at seven-thirty in the morning to get a status report.

I called John Hocking and asked him to announce Cox's confession to the press. I asked him to personally deliver the news to Melinda Brown and Jamal Jackson. I said, "I'm not sure what impact that will have on their protests, but I want them to hear about it before the eleven o'clock news carries it."

Hocking said, "That should take the wind out of their sail. I hear BLM and BAP are demanding the council fire you."

"Yes, so this isn't over yet, John. Keep up your good work."

"What do you think the council is going to do?"

"They'll do what's best for this city. Whatever they decide to do, I support them on it."

"Whatever happens, Jed, I think you've done a fine job."

"Thanks, John."

32

When I arrived home, Ashley Rand's Mercedes was parked in my driveway. I walked into my living room and noticed that the rear sliding glass door that led out to the dock was ajar. On the kitchenette table was a bucket with an open bottle of Chardonnay on ice. A clean wine glass sat next to the bucket.

I took the bottle from the bucket, poured the glass half full and found Ashley sitting at the end of the dock. It was half-past-ten o'clock, and the chanting and noise from the protesters in Riverside Park across the river was quieter. There were still upwards of two hundred protestors in the park, no doubt waiting for the local and national television news coverage at eleven o'clock. If there was going to be violence, the crowd across the way didn't seem to be moving in that direction.

Ashley stood as I approached. She wore white jean shorts and a low-cut, tight-fitting black tank top. She'd pulled her black hair back into a ponytail and wore no makeup. She put her hands around my neck and pulled me into a warm kiss.

She stepped back and said, "I almost gave up on you. You look exhausted."

"But the big news of the evening is Cox confessed in exchange for a plea deal."

We sat on the bench together, leaving room between us for our wine glasses. The air was thick with moisture, and the sounds of the river were soothing.

She said, "Have you heard anything from the city council yet?"

"How did you know about the meeting?"

"It is all over national cable news, and the worst-kept secret in town." She put a knee up on the bench to turn toward me. "What do you think the council will do? We should have heard something by now."

"I suspect, given the threats that Jamal Jackson and Melinda Brown made to the council, that they'll do what's best for the city and ask me to leave."

Ashely took a sip of her wine and asked, "How is that best for the city?"

"The prospect of BLM and BAP doing to Coronado Beach what they did in Ferguson and Milwaukee must be uppermost in their minds. They really don't have a choice. If this turns violent because they keep me on the job, then the mob will blame the council. They can't afford to let that happen."

"That isn't right. You've done nothing wrong."

"It doesn't matter. The council can't put the entire city at risk over one person. It would be irresponsible to do anything else."

"Eddy was such a fool. He should have never had anything to do with Cox. None of this would have happened. He set into motion circumstances that led to two murders."

I said, "He made bad choices. First, he chose to do business with someone as unstable as Sabatini. Then he fell in love with the wrong person."

"I appreciate your effort to try to insulate Eddy from prosecution."

"In truth, it was Cahill and the ASA who decided Eddy's fate. If it had been my call, I'd have charged him. When Cox asked Eddy to launder money, Eddy knew what he was doing was wrong. He was an officer of the court. If anyone knew the law, he did. The fact that he skated on the laundering charge bothers me. But I'm glad it was not my decision to make. I can look Nicole in the eye and tell her I had nothing to do with the plea deal."

"I told Nicole that you helped Eddy. Eddy is under the impression that you used your influence with Cahill to gloss over his involvement. I don't want either of them to know otherwise. Promise me."

"Ashley, I can't make that promise. Eddy's deal with the ASA may have shielded him from prosecution, but it won't shield him from legal challenges."

"Like what?"

"You know better than I do that if the Bar Association gets a whiff of this, they could bring him up on ethics charges. If they decide to pursue an investigation, at a minimum they could suspend his license while they conduct a probe. In the worst case, they could disbar him."

"It may not come to that."

"Ashley, this case has drawn national and international attention. Once all this paperwork reaches the court, the press will eventually bring everything out into the open. If Nicole finds out that you or I withheld the truth about Eddy from her, that isn't going to end well."

"Jed, Nicole adores you. I don't want to do anything to change that."

"I don't either, but I don't want a relationship with her that's based on deception. Nicole is a smart girl. She's entitled to know what's going on. She deserves to know the truth."

"And you're willing to risk what that knowledge might do to our relationship? As much as Nicole likes you, she absolutely loves her father, and she's very protective of him. She might take her father's side and look on everyone connected with this as the enemy. If that happens, that could seriously affect us."

"I can't control that. As I said, Cahill and the ASA made that deal with Eddy. And while I didn't have anything to do with the deal, I was involved. Nicole will figure that out very quickly. The question is, would it be better for her to find out about it from us or from something that she reads online?"

"Let me think on that."

I said, "Eddy should be the one to tell her what happened. How he explains all this to her will determine how things will progress with us."

"I agree—that's a better way to deal with this. I'll talk to him." Ashley stood and picked up both of our wine glasses. "Sit tight. Let me get us some more wine."

Ashley left me on the dock, reflecting on Eddy's involvement. If they disbarred Eddy and he could no longer practice law, how would that affect Ashley? If she took over Eddy's law practice and began representing criminal cases in Coronado Beach, it could create conflicts of interest for both Ashley and me. I reasoned that that was the worst-case scenario. And I was not prepared to do anything that would change my relationship with her.

Ashley returned with AJ, who was carrying a can of beer in a koozie. "Look who I found lurking around."

"AJ, come join us," I said.

Ashley handed me a refilled glass of wine. We all held our beverages up in a silent toast.

"Let's go inside so we can all sit," I said.

Firestorm

AJ said, "I've been sitting on my ass all evening. You two sit, and I'll stand. I've news on the city council meeting, and then I should scoot."

Ashley and I sat on the bench, and AJ paced back and forth on the dock.

"That was an interesting council meeting," he said. "My respect for Councilman Banks has risen dramatically. For beginners, he has enormous respect for you. He reacted poorly to Jamal Jackson's threats. He didn't feel the council should give in to his demands. He told the council that he wanted to wait until after ten o'clock before the council voted. He wanted to see if there was any sign that Jackson would follow through on his threat of violence. We called Tom Morris and asked him to give us a report on the crowd and whether there was any evidence that they were preparing to break through the barricades at Riverside Park. Morris told us that the crowd began to thin when the news reported that Cox had confessed. Banks said he thought Jackson was all talk, and since he'd backed down on demanding to have protestors at City Hall and demanding we fire Jarret, Banks was convinced that Jackson would back down on his demand that we fire you. So, we waited to see if anything materialized. Then Morris told us the crowds were thinning.

"The council decided that they weren't going to do anything. There was no vote of confidence. The council adjourned. It was incredible. I called Morris on my way home, and he told me that protesters remained but that after the eleven o'clock news, he felt like the crowds would begin to disperse. We will never know whether the council has confidence in you or not." He held up his beer then drank heavily of it.

"Any sign of Jamal Jackson?" I asked.

"Morris says not. I'm hoping since there will be no trial, everything will blow over. We'll see."

I said, "Thanks, AJ."

"Don't thank me, thank Banks. He had the wisdom to wait the situation out rather than panic. He told the council that there are times when doing nothing is appropriate. It was wise not to take a vote. Individual council members were afraid. Had there been a vote, some may have voted against you. After ten o'clock, when nothing happened and Banks suggested doing nothing, it took the pressure off to decide. It was brilliant. We will see whether that was the right thing to do."

AJ finished his beer. "I got to go. Us old people need our sleep. But I'll say one more thing. What saved the day was your efforts to collaborate with the Black community and gain their trust. Banks told me to tell you that he appreciated your willingness to sacrifice yourself to save the city from harm."

AJ gave Ashley a hug and wished us a good night.

After he left, Ashley took a sip of wine and asked me, "Do you think this is over?"

"I don't know. We will know more tomorrow. We have a press conference at nine a.m. If Eddy hadn't come through when he did, I think the situation could have been violent. His testimony was crucial. The fact that we were able to charge Cox so quickly helped relieve pressure. When we announced that Cox had confessed, taking away the need for a trial, we lowered the pressure more." I pointed across the river to Riverside Park. I looked at my watch. It was eleven-fifteen. "It looks like the crowd at the park is thinning out."

"You thought they'd vote no confidence, didn't you?" Ashley asked.

"If I'd been on the council, that's what I would have done."

"There's no getting around the politics in your job."

I said, "There's a part of me that hoped for a no confidence vote. I'm a homicide investigator in chief's clothing. I'm no politician. There's too much drama in that."

"So, why do you continue to do it? Cahill would snap you up in a second and find a place for you in the FDLE."

"That's a good question. The former chief's incompetent leadership created a nightmare for this department. Grizzle trusted no one, and he was such a wuss, he wouldn't make decisions either. He never got in trouble because he never did anything. In the last three years, the people in the PD have grown and come into their own because I freed them to make decisions, and their confidence has grown because they know I trust them. Yes, I could quit. I could work with FDLE, but the next chief might reverse all of that. I can't let that happen. These are good people who enjoy their work, and they're good at what they do."

"Yet you were willing to resign."

"If my staying in the job was the reason for the destruction of the town, I couldn't have lived with that. Who would have benefited? Certainly not the department."

"The department is better with you in it, Jed. And my life is better with you in it."

"Are you staying tonight?" I asked.

"I have Nicole. Eddy came over to stay with her until I got home. I promised him I wouldn't be late. I've stayed longer than I should. I've decided to take your advice. Eddy and I need to talk to Nicole about what has happened. It is better that she hears it from us. It is better to find out how she reacts now versus later."

"Thanks for being here tonight."

She stood up to leave.

I asked, "I have one question for you. How did you get Eddy to come forward when he did?"

"I threatened to file for sole custody of Nicole if he didn't."

She hugged me, kissed me and said she could make it to her car without escort.

33

When I arrived in my office at seven-thirty in the morning, Sergeant Johnson had already pulled extra chairs into my office. The entire staff was there, including Jim Cahill. The only person missing was Leslie Downs.

I encouraged Tom Morris to begin the briefing.

Tom sat at one of the chairs around the conference table, while the others formed a large circle around the room.

Morris said, "Jed, before we start, word has reached us that the council took no action against you last night, despite the threats from BLM and BAP. I know I speak for everyone in the room when I say how glad we are that you're here this morning, still wearing that badge on your belt."

Everyone clapped and affirmed Morris's statement.

"I just checked Riverside Park," Morris continued. "The number of protesters is about half what they were yesterday. The shuttles are still running from the airport staging area into town, but they're half full. So far, everything is peaceful."

"How about BLM and BAP? Any sign of them this morning?" I asked.

"Not so far."

I asked John Hocking, "Do you have a press conference set up for this morning?"

"Yes, I took the liberty of setting it up for nine-thirty. When we alerted the press to Cox's confession last night, we didn't supply enough detail. It isn't even eight a.m., and news outlets have besieged me with calls."

"Would you find Councilman Banks and ask him if he'd attend the press conference? A supporting statement from him would go a long way to calm the community."

34

It was moments before the presser, and I stood inside the front door, waiting for Gabriel Banks to arrive. Hocking had placed a lectern a few steps outside the lobby door, and the various news organizations had crammed their microphones and recording devices on top of it. Banks navigated around the scrum of reporters, and I opened the door to let him in.

"Good morning, Mr. Banks," I said. "I'm pleased you could come." We backed away from the front door and into the lobby.

Banks asked, "Have you heard anything from Jamal Jackson?"

"No, sir. Nothing from Ms. Brown either."

"I was looking for them as I walked here from home. I was praying they'd have pulled up stakes and moved on."

"I was hoping you might make a statement this morning. I understand from Commander Morris that while there are still protestors from out of town arriving at the airport, people from our community are out in large numbers, and they're angry. A word from you would go a long way to restoring peace."

Councilman Banks looked down at his shoes, then up at me. "I'm sorry, Chief, but I won't do that." He turned and looked out the lobby door and turned back to me. "After Cox shot Robinson, you came to me and asked for my help. We faced the prospect of destructive riots, looting and the loss of our town—our home. I couldn't let that happen. That would have divided our city and set back our efforts to bridge the racial gap for a decade.

"I was able to work behind the scenes and convince the Black leaders that if we remained silent, BLM and BAP would interpret that as support for violence to further their cause. We all agreed that we had to do something. You were wise to involve us at such an early stage. And this is consistent with the way you've approached us since you became chief.

"At the same time, even though we've made progress reducing the racial tension in Coronado Beach, we've a long way to go. Those folks in Riverside Park are angry. You and I understand there was no racial motive in the murder of Robinson. But they don't. They see it as just another example, like so many others, of Black men killed by White cops because of the color of their skin. You've no idea how deeply rooted this resentment is and how difficult it is to reverse two plus centuries of discrimination and mistreatment.

"Even though we were able to work together to avoid violence, and even though I respect and applaud what you're trying to do for the Black people here, we aren't on the same side. I represent the Black folks of this city. Their hopes and dreams are my hopes and dreams. You and I are on opposite sides of many issues. My speaking at this press conference would send the wrong message. If I'm going to stand anywhere, it will be with the protesters in Riverside Park. I hope you understand."

I said, "I understand." And I did.

Banks reached up and squeezed my shoulder, then walked out the door and wended his way toward Riverside Park.

Firestorm

Jim Cahill did a splendid job with the press conference. Downs, Jarret and I stood behind Cahill at the lectern. Normally the FDLE didn't discuss ongoing cases, and FDLE's public role was a rarity. It spoke to the seriousness of the case and the concern for the potential for violence. The presser lasted an hour, and Cahill discussed as much of the case and Cox's confession as the ASA would allow.

After the presser, I had an impromptu staff meeting. I invited Cahill to attend, but he begged off, saying that he still had loose ends on the Cox case to tie up. I invited him to the house for a drink later that evening, but he declined, saying, "Sandy told me that she'd forgotten what I looked like. I took that to mean that she's had enough of me playing cops and robbers and expected me to take her out to dinner."

It took less than twenty minutes to get status reports. Morris summed up where we were in one sentence. "Until the protesters are gone, we're still on high alert."

After the staff meeting was over, Leslie Downs hung back. I assumed it had something to do with the Cox case. But after she stood there for a moment in silence, I asked, "What's up?"

"I didn't want to discuss this with you until we got past this crisis."

More silence.

I said, "Okay..."

"My Dad is retiring." Downs' father was the chief of police in Daytona Beach.

"That's terrific. I'm sure you're pleased for him. When will it happen?"

"As soon as they find a replacement. Which is why I want to talk to you. He wants me to put my name in the hat to replace him. He's heading up the search committee."

"How are you feeling about that?"

"Honestly, I don't know. I think it would be a long shot. There are tons of chiefs from all over the country who would kill for a post like that. I just don't have any experience. And my father will push for me as his replacement. It has nepotism written all over it in capital letters. You parachuted into the chief's job. You understand the resentment the senior staff here had when Jarret dropped you into the top spot. The fact that I'm the chief's daughter and a woman without command experience...well... That would add to the resistance I'd have to overcome. I'm not sure I want that."

Losing Downs would be a major blow to me and the department.

"Leslie, you're an excellent investigator. You're an intelligent, gifted leader and administrator. You're ambitious and driven, and you've the force of personality needed to survive life in the hotseat. You're so impressive, all you need to do is show up for an interview and you'll get the job. Yes, if they select you, there would be opposition. But then, once they see how talented you are, their attitudes will change. I'm with your father. You should apply. You'll get an enthusiastic reference from me, if that's what you want."

"How could I leave after you said all these wonderful things about me?"

"I think you'd make an excellent chief. Obviously, your father thinks you're qualified, or he wouldn't have encouraged you to apply."

Firestorm

"Like I said, I don't know what I want to do. The position would have significant responsibility and stress. I'm happy here. I love working with you. At the same time, there are very few female chiefs in the state. I'd like to add to their number. You understand that, right?"

"I do. I appreciate the classy way you managed this. Does anyone else in the department know?"

"No. You're the first person."

"Can we keep it that way until you make a decision?"

"Of course. I can't tell you how much I appreciate the kind things you said to me." She came forward and hugged me, then turned and left my office.

I sat down at the conference table and pondered what it would mean for the department if she left. It occurred to me how different Downs and I were. She was driven; I was not. I'd have been content to do the job they'd originally hired me to do, homicide detective. There was something in Downs that made her exceptional, a quality essential to greatness. Since I'd become chief, Downs had become a bright star, not only in our PD but also in the law enforcement community in the county. While she was content in her current situation, she'd quickly outgrow her position and need more challenging work. I'd no doubt that her drive to succeed would propel her to apply for the job.

After the press conference, I was ready to take the afternoon off, get a cold beer out of the refrigerator, and sit on the dock and decompress. I decided that it would be wise to stick around until it was clear that the crisis was over. By late afternoon, there were only stragglers in Riverside Park, the crowds replaced with city workers raking up vitriolic signs and pamphlets. Commander

Morris ordered the discontinuation of bus service after all the vehicles at the airport had connected with their owners. City workers removed all the barricades to the entrances of the city. We transported Cory Cox to the Volusia County jail, where he'd remain until the ASA disposed of his case.

All afternoon I'd been thinking about Ashley, Nicole and Eddy and how the Rands would treat the open wound of Eddy's involvement with Cory Cox. I'd been expecting a call from her and had tried to reach her three times during the afternoon, but the calls had gone to voicemail. This was unusual. She always took my calls. If she were on a call or in a meeting, she'd text me immediately and tell me she'd call "in a few." I did the same. So I left the office and headed home with Ashley on my mind.

35

At home, I showered and changed into cutoffs, a T-shirt and flip-flops. I grabbed a beer out of the refrigerator and, as I opened the sliding glass door, I noticed AJ McFarland sitting at the end of the dock. I also noted black storm clouds gathering to the west. It was every bit of ninety degrees, and the humidity was so oppressive that I broke out in a sweat before I reached AJ. I could see Riverside Park across the river and, aside from a couple of fishers casting bait into the river, the park was empty.

AJ had a beer in a New York Yankees koozie in his hand. Wearing white shorts, a tennis shirt and flip-flops. When I stood beside him, I noticed a small red soft cooler by his feet, which told me this was going to be a two-beer get-together. He never brought more than the one he was drinking and a second if he intended to talk for a while. I sat down on the bench next to him. I could hear thunder off in the distance, but it was still miles away.

AJ said, "You live a charmed life, my boy. If you were a cat with nine lives, I'd say you've used up most of them." He pulled a handkerchief from his pants pocket and wiped the sweat from his face.

"Thanks once again for all your support. Without it, the council would have fired me the week after I arrived here."

"You owe me, Jed. You know that, right?"

"Yes, I owe you. Big time."

He turned in his seat and pointed back to the house. "Tear down this house. I feel like Ronald Reagan standing at the Berlin Wall. Tear down this house."

I laughed, and then I couldn't stop. Every time we got together, he made snarky comments about the house to the point it became a running joke between us. Even after all my efforts to clean it up and paint the outside and make it presentable, it was still the ugliest house on the street.

He said, "I'll tell you what I'll do. I'll pay the cost to tear the house down and haul it off. Your property value will increase by one hundred and fifty thousand. And you don't have to do anything, just sit with me and drink beer while they demolish this ugly, godawful eyesore."

"Why don't you tell me how you really feel, AJ."

We both laughed.

He held up his beer, and I tapped my bottle against his koozie.

I said, "I'm holding out for a new home. I'm thinking by next year, I will piss you off so bad that you'll cough up the money to build a new house for me. Think about how much it will increase the value of *your* property."

"I think Ashley would probably help me pay for it."

Ashley appeared behind us. "What am I going to help you pay for?"

"Tearing down this mess of a house and building a new one."

Both AJ and I stood to make room on the two-person bench for Ashley. She sat down where I had been sitting.

Firestorm

I said, "Let me go get a chair so we can all sit," and I started down the dock toward the house.

AJ said, "No, no, no, I was just leaving! After today, I'm whipped." He said to Ashley, "I just wanted to come over and pat Wonder Boy on the back for surviving another catastrophe."

AJ picked up his soft cooler. Ashley stood and hugged him. I was going to tell him that he didn't have to go, but Ashley was wearing pajamas, she had pulled her hair back into a disheveled bun, and she wore no makeup. Something was up.

"Ashley, can I get you a glass of wine or a beer?" I asked.

"I can't stay long."

I sat down next to her. She folded her hands in her lap. She looked straight forward, avoiding eye contact.

"What's wrong?"

"This will be hard to hear, Jed."

"So just spill it."

"I can't continue my relationship with you." Tears streamed down her cheeks into her lap. "I'm emotionally exhausted. Eddy, Nicole and I spent the entire afternoon going over everything that happened. I don't have the energy to go over all of it with you now, but I felt I should tell you now in person. I didn't want to do it over the phone."

I felt gut punched. I was too shocked to say anything.

She continued, "There's a ton of family drama in this, but in the end, I realized how quickly our relationship collided with your very public role as chief of police. As soon as the press starts digging down into this and learns that we've been in a relationship and I'm the ex-wife of someone connected to the case...well, you can imagine how the public will view that. And when you told me you'd have arrested Eddy for his role, even though Cox was blackmailing him, I couldn't handle that. I knew that your attitude about Eddy would interfere with your relationship with him and Nicole."

She looked me in the eye for the first time. "While I'm in love with you, I'm not in love with your job. This Cox fiasco convinced me I was too close to it. You'd be a constant reminder of the ugliness Nicole and I have just gone through. It's too much, Jed. It's too much." She stood.

"That's it? Aren't we going to talk about it?"

"Yes, we can talk about it. But not tonight, please. But I'll say this. It will not change my mind."

She hugged and kissed me and marched down the dock, and around the side of the house.. Soon, I heard the engine of her car start up, and lightning cracked across the river in Riverside Park. I could hear the rain coming and barely made it to the door before the downpour was so hard, I couldn't see the end of the dock from the slider.

Epilogue

Since the Robinson shooting didn't produce violence, looting, political drama or a trial, news coverage evaporated. The sentencing hearing lasted long enough for the court to accept the plea bargain and make it official. Cox received a life sentence with no opportunity for parole.

Ashley Rand and I had a difficult discussion a week after she announced the end of our relationship. Ashley was a warm, beautiful woman, inside and out. There were so many qualities about her that made our breakup difficult. We talked for two hours, but nothing I said would change her mind.

In the months that followed, the Bar Association never investigated Eddy Rand, nor was he written about in the press. There was absolutely no fallout for him following the finalization of Cox's plea agreement. All of Ashley's fears about Eddy's involvement becoming public and affecting our relationship never happened. She and I met one more time, and I pointed this out to her and sought to reconcile, without success. She finally settled on the fact that my job was the single factor in her decision. She had quit practicing criminal law when she and Eddy divorced. After the Cox case, she'd realized that she was replacing Eddy with someone even more deeply involved with criminals.

When I met with her the last time, I came close to asking her if it would change things between us if I resigned. In retrospect, I was glad I'd held my tongue.

The Cox affair was toxic, and there was no way to change that chemistry for the Rand family. And it was impossible for me to erase my involvement in it. In the end, I was still resentful that Eddy Rand had come through this unscathed. I was convinced that when Cox had confessed, he'd covered up for Eddy, minimizing his involvement in the conspiracy. At first, I didn't want to admit how strong my feelings were toward Eddy. After my second talk with Ashley, I knew I wouldn't fit into their world. And I knew that while I was willing to resign as chief, I was not ready to give up law enforcement. It was all I knew, and I was too young to retire. It was part of who I was. I couldn't change that for her. I couldn't change that for anyone.

-End-

Contact Information

To receive updates and news on Bill Cronin's books, "like" his Facebook page.
http://facebook.com/billcroninwrite.
You can contact the author directly:
billcroninwrite@gmail.com

Bill Cronin's Other Books

Stand-Alone Novels
Available as e-books.
Dial Tone, 2012
The Tainted Lady, 2014

Jack McNamara Chronicles
All available as e-books and paperback.

The Song of the Mockingbird, Book 1, 2013
Ruby's Story, Book 2, 2014
Letting Go, Book 3, 2015
Joe and the Governor, Book 4, 2016

Jed McCain Mysteries
All available as e-books, audiobooks and paperback.

Night Fire, Book 1, 2017
Playing with Fire, Book 2, 2017
Firestorm, Book 3, 2025